英汉双语国学经典
The Bilingual Reading of the Chinese Classics

翟理斯英译本

# 古今诗选

CHINESE POETRY IN ENGLISH VERSE

著者/（汉）刘　彻　等
译者/（英）翟理斯
注译/朱爱清　鲍　杰

中州古籍出版社
·郑州·

## 图书在版编目(CIP)数据

古今诗选:英汉对照/(汉)刘彻等著;(英)翟理斯译. —郑州:中州古籍出版社,2021.9
ISBN 978-7-5348-8452-8

Ⅰ.①古… Ⅱ.①刘… ②翟… Ⅲ.①古典诗歌-诗集-中国-英、汉 Ⅳ.①I222

中国版本图书馆CIP数据核字(2019)第027232号

GUJIN SHIXUAN

### 古今诗选

策划编辑:吴　浩
责任编辑:李晓文　翟　楠
责任校对:李瑞瑞

| 出版社 | 中州古籍出版社(地址:郑州市郑东新区祥盛街27号6层邮编:450016　电话:0371-65788693) |
|---|---|
| 发行单位 | 河南省新华书店发行集团有限公司 |
| 承印单位 | 河南印之星印务有限公司 |
| 开　　本 | 640mm×960mm　1/16 |
| 印　　张 | 14.25 |
| 字　　数 | 220千字 |
| 版　　次 | 2021年9月第1版 |
| 印　　次 | 2021年9月第1次印刷 |
| 定　　价 | 35.00元 |

本书如有印装质量问题,请与出版社调换。

# 前　　言

"英汉双语国学经典"系列丛书的英译本,选用的是近现代一些西方著名汉学家的汉籍英译本,《古今诗选》亦是其中之一。

《古今诗选》是英国著名汉学家翟里斯(Herbert A. Giles,1845~1935)选译的中国古诗集。翟里斯被誉为英国汉学领域"三大星座"之一,他在中国语言、文化、文学研究方面造诣颇深,著述甚多,两度荣获法兰西学院儒莲汉籍国际翻译奖。翟里斯的"韵体译诗"对后世影响很大,所翻译的中国古诗很是"雅致"。尽管有人对翟里斯翻译的中国古诗提出"因韵害义"的质疑,但这并不影响西方读者对翟里斯译作的喜爱。本书所选古诗按照创作时间先后为序进行编排,选取作品上自远古铭文的"人莫踬于山,而踬于垤",下至宋明的"春色满园关不住,一枝红杏出墙来""大将南征胆气豪,腰横秋水雁翎刀"。

本书底本选自伦敦 Lodon Bernard Quartch 和上海 Kelly and Walsh, Ld. 于1898年联合出版的 *CHINESE POETRY IN ENGLISH VERSE* 英语版本。基于保留英语韵体诗的韵律需要,在本书的编辑整理中,有些古体英语没做改动,以存翟氏作品原貌。例如 you 的单复数变化和各种格：thou 即单数 you,ye 即复数 you,thine 即宾格 yours； o'er 即 over 的缩写,'Tis 即 It is 的缩写；其他古体如 ope 即 open 的诗意用法等。此外,还有个别单词用的是其他语种,以及有确系译者误译、错译的地方,编者均在文中做了注释。

本书采用英汉对照的排版方式,单页是英语,双页是汉语,既有汉语古文,又有现代汉语释文,还有英语,方便读者三种文本对照阅读。

　　由于编者水平有限,书中难免会有疏漏不足,敬请读者朋友批评指正。

编　者

# 目 录 contents

诗经·将仲子　TO A YOUNG GENTLEMAN　/ 2
诗经·氓　TO A MAN　/ 4
诗经·蟋蟀（节选）　THE CRICKET　/ 10
击壤歌　THE HUSBANDMAN'S SONG　/ 10
尧戒　YAO'S ADVICE　/ 12
盥盘铭　INSCRIPTION ON A WASH-BASIN　/ 12
青青河畔草　NEGLECTED　/ 14
涉江采芙蓉　PARTED　/ 14
秋风辞　AMARI ALIQUID　/ 16
落叶哀蝉曲　GONE　/ 18
怨歌行　THE AUTUMN FAN　/ 18
生年不满百　CARPE DIEM　/ 20
驱车上东门　THE ELIXIR OF LIFE　/ 22
杂诗　A FIRST-BORN　/ 24
室思（其三）　AN ABSENT HUSBAND　/ 26
短歌行　ON THE DEATH OF HIS FATHER　/ 28
七步诗　THE BROTHERS　/ 30
吴楚歌　LOVERS PARTED　/ 32

1

车遥遥篇　AFTER PARTING　　　／32

拟古（其四）　SIC TRANSIT　　／34

拟古（其五）　A RECLUSE　　　／36

读《山海经》（其五）　A PRAYER　／38

拟行路难（其三）　ALONE　　　／40

赠逸民诗（其十一）　ULTIMATE CAUSES　／40

效阮公诗（其十）　FORGOTTEN　／42

人日思归（节选）　ANTICIPATION　／44

野望　IN ABSENCE　　／44

滕王阁诗　ICHABOD　　／46

登幽州台歌　REGRETS　　／48

感遇（其十九）　AGAINST IDOLS　／48

回乡偶书　THE RETURN　　／50

和赵员外桂阳桥遇佳人　A VISION　／52

望月怀远　BY MOONLIGHT　／52

宿业师山房待丁大不至　WAITING　／54

夏日南亭怀辛大　IN DREAMLAND　／56

宿建德江　AT ANCHOR　／56

罢相作　OUT OF OFFICE　／58

竹里馆　OVERLOOKED　／60

山中送别　GOODBYE　／60

杂诗　A RENCONTRE　／62

送别　GOODBYE TO MENG HAO-JAN　／62

黄鹤楼　HOME LONGINGS　／64

咏萤火　TO A FIREFLY　　　/ 64

江夏别宋之悌　AT PARTING　　　/ 66

静夜思　NIGHT THOUGHTS　　　/ 68

独坐敬亭山　COMPANIONS　　　/ 68

秋思　FROM A BELVIDERE　　　/ 70

乌夜啼　FOR HER HUSBAND　　　/ 70

春日醉起言志　"THE BEST OF LIFE IS BUT..."　　　/ 72

金陵酒肆留别　FAREWELL BY THE RIVER　　　/ 74

送孟浩然之广陵　GONE　　　/ 76

秋风词　NO INSPIRATION　　　/ 76

夜泊牛渚怀古　GENERAL HSIEH AN　　　/ 78

姑孰十咏·丹阳湖（节选）　A SNAP-SHOT　　　/ 78

送友人　A FAREWELL　　　/ 80

古朗月行　BOYHOOD FANCIES　　　/ 82

玉阶怨　FROM THE PALACE　　　/ 84

山中问答　THE POET　　　/ 84

怨情　TEARS　　　/ 86

宫中行乐词（其一）　A FAVOURITE　　　/ 86

客中作　IN EXILE　　　/ 88

秋浦歌（其十五）　IN A MIRROR　　　/ 88

月下独酌（其一）　LAST WORDS　　　/ 90

绝句二首（其二）　IN ABSENCE　　　/ 92

落日　WINE　　　/ 92

月夜忆舍弟　TO HIS BROTHER　　　/ 94

江村　HOME JOYS　　　／ 96

琴台　SSU-MA HSIANG-JU　　　／ 98

题张氏隐居二首（其一）　THE HERMIT　　　／ 98

曲江二首（其一）　SOLO CHI SEGUE CIÒ CHE PIACE
　　　　É SAGGIO　　　／ 100

曲江二首（其二）　DUM RES ET AETAS　　　／ 102

陪诸贵公子丈八沟携妓纳凉，晚际遇雨二首（其一）　A PICNIC　　　／ 104

石壕吏　THE PRESSGANG　　　／ 104

绝句漫兴九首（其五）　SPRING JOYS　　　／ 108

题破山寺后禅院　DHYANA　　　／ 108

宫中词　IN THE HAREM　　　／ 110

别卢秦卿　OH STAY　　　／ 112

春思二首（其一）　SPRING SORROWS　　　／ 112

滁州西涧　SUPERSEDED　　　／ 114

秋夜寄邱员外　REMEMBRANCES　　　／ 114

寄李儋元锡　A PROMISE　　　／ 116

登总持阁　BUDDHISM　　　／ 118

凉州词二首（其一）　A REASON FAIR　　　／ 118

秋日　LONELY　　　／ 120

经漂母墓　THE WASHERWOMAN'S GRAVE　　　／ 120

伊州歌　AT DAWN　　　／ 122

同王徵君湘中有怀句　NOSTALGIA　　　／ 124

闺怨　AT THE WARS　　　／ 124

芙蓉楼送辛渐　A MESSAGE　　　／ 126

苏氏别业　A GROTTO　　/ 128

题都城南庄　A RETROSPECT　　/ 128

玉台体　HOPE　　/ 130

病鹞　THE WOUNDED FALCON　　/ 132

读皇甫湜公安园池诗书其后二首(其二)　HOURS OF IDLENESS　　/ 136

感春四首(其四)　DISCONTENT　　/ 136

杂诗四首(其一)　HUMANITY　　/ 140

杂曲歌辞·少年乐　NEAERA'S TANGLES　　/ 142

秋风引　SUMMER DYING　　/ 142

和乐天春词　THE ODALISQUE　　/ 144

后宫词　DESERTED　　/ 146

行宫　AT AN OLD PALACE　　/ 146

宫怨　A CAST-OFF FAVOURITE　　/ 148

节妇吟·寄东平李司空师道　THE CHASTE WIFE'S REPLY　　/ 148

城东早春　TASTE　　/ 150

怅诗　A LOST LOVE　　/ 152

金谷园　THE OLD PLACE　　/ 152

赠别二首(其二)　THE LAST NIGHT　　/ 154

七夕　LOVERS PARTED　　/ 154

登乐游原　THE NIGHT COMES　　/ 156

夜雨寄北　SOUVENIRS　　/ 156

社日　A SPRING FEAST　　/ 158

登山　ESCAPE　　/ 158

井栏砂宿遇夜客　ON HIGHWAYMEN　　/ 160

春晴　A STORM　　／ 160

即景　SUMMER BEGINS　　／ 162

落花　LOVE'S SPRINGTIME　　／ 162

江楼感旧　WHERE ARE THEY?　　／ 164

除夜宿石头驿　NEW YEAR'S EVE AT AN INN　　／ 164

婕妤春怨　SPRETAE INJURIA FORMAE　　／ 166

秋日湖上　MUSING　　／ 166

闻邻家理筝　MY NEIGHBOUR　　／ 168

贫女　THE SEMPSTRESS　　／ 170

春夕　THE TRAVELLER　　／ 172

金缕衣　GOLDEN SANDS　　／ 172

旅游伤春　WANDERJAHRE　　／ 176

听筝　MUSIC HATH CHARMS　　／ 176

寄王舍人竹楼　IN RETIREMENT　　／ 178

春怨　THE SPINSTER　　／ 178

效崔国辅体四首（其一）　CONTEMPLATION　　／ 180

渡汉江　HOMEWARD　　／ 182

陇西行　AN OATH　　／ 182

寄人　TO AN ABSENT FAIR ONE　　／ 184

归隐　DISILLUSIONED　　／ 184

夜宿山寺　'TWIXT HEAVEN AND EARTH　　／ 186

戏答元珍　CONSOLATION　　／ 188

插花吟　A STRUGGLE　　／ 190

有约　WAITING　　／ 192

清明　ANNUAL WORSHIP AT TOMBS　　／192

夜直　A WHITE NIGHT　　／194

题淮南寺　INSOUCIANCE　　／196

春日偶成　SPRING FANCIES　　／196

春宵　SPRING NIGHTS　　／198

花影　WHIGS AND TORIES　　／198

秋千　SWINGING　　／200

初夏游张园　SUMMER　　／202

游园不值　AT A PARK GATE　　／202

冷泉　A MOUNTAIN BROOK　　／204

送春　THE THIRD MOON　　／204

清明日对酒　WORSHIP, AND AFTER　　／206

蚕妇吟　AT HIS CLUB　　／208

暮春即事　AT HIS BOOKS　　／208

晨诣祥符寺　AT A MOUNTAIN MONASTERY　　／210

绝句　OMNES EODEM　　／210

暮春江上送别　TO HER LOVER　　／212

送毛伯温　TO GENERAL MAO　　／212

古今诗选

## 诗经·将仲子

将仲子兮,无逾我里,无折我树杞。岂敢爱之?
畏我父母。仲可怀也,父母之言亦可畏也。

将仲子兮,无逾我墙,无折我树桑。岂敢爱之?
畏我诸兄。仲可怀也,诸兄之言亦可畏也。

将仲子兮,无逾我园,无折我树檀。岂敢爱之?
畏人之多言。仲可怀也,人之多言亦可畏也。

【今译】

　　仲子哥哥呀,请不要翻越我家的门户,别弄折了我家的杞树。哪是舍不得杞树呢?实在是害怕我的父母。我很思念我的仲子哥哥,但父母的话也会让我担心和害怕。
　　仲子哥哥呀,请不要翻越我家的围墙,别弄折了我家的桑树。哪是舍不得桑树呢?实在是害怕我的兄长们。我很思念我的仲子哥哥,但是兄长们的话也会让我担心和害怕。
　　仲子哥哥呀,请不要踏过我家的菜园,别弄折了我家的檀树。哪是舍不得檀树呢?实在是害怕邻人的闲话。我很思念我的仲子哥哥,但是邻人的闲话也会让我担心和害怕。

## TO A YOUNG GENTLEMAN

Don't come in, sir, please!
Don't break my willow-trees!
Not that that would very much grieve me;
But alack-a-day! what would my parents say?
And love you as I may,
I cannot bear to think what that would be.

Don't cross my wall, sir, please!
Don't spoil my mulberry-trees!
Not that that would very much grieve me;
But alack-a-day! what would my brothers say?
And love you as I may,
I cannot bear to think what that would be.

Keep outside, sir, please!
Don't spoil my sandal-trees!
Not that that would very much grieve me;
But alack-a-day! what the world would say!
And love you as I may,
I cannot bear to think what that would be.

# 诗经·氓

　　氓之蚩蚩，抱布贸丝。匪来贸丝，来即我谋。送子涉淇，至于顿丘。匪我愆期，子无良媒。将子无怒，秋以为期。乘彼垝垣，以望复关。不见复关，泣涕涟涟。既见复关，载笑载言。尔卜尔筮，体无咎言。以尔车来，以我贿迁。

　　桑之未落，其叶沃若。于嗟鸠兮，无食桑葚。于嗟女兮，无与士耽。士之耽兮，犹可说也。女之耽兮，不可说也。桑之落矣，其黄而陨。自我徂尔，三岁食贫。淇水汤汤，渐车帷裳。女也不爽，士贰其行。士也罔极，二三其德。三岁为妇，靡室劳矣。夙兴夜寐，靡有朝矣。言既遂矣，至于暴矣。兄弟不知，咥其笑矣。静言思之，躬自悼矣。及尔偕老，老使我怨。淇则有岸，隰则有泮。总角之宴，言笑晏晏。信誓旦旦，不思其反。反是不思，亦已焉哉。

【今译】

　　满脸笑容的年轻小伙子啊，抱着布匹来换丝。其实他并不是真心来换丝哟，不过是找个借口来找我商量结婚的事啊。我送郎君过了那淇河啊，到了顿丘仍依依不舍。不是我故意拖延婚期呀，实在是你没有找到好媒人来说媒。请郎君不要发怒啊，我们就把婚期约定在秋天吧。登上那倒塌的墙壁，遥望着你所在的复关。复关太遥远，我看不见啊，不禁流下思念的涕泪。看到郎君从复关来啊，我不禁又变得喜笑颜开。

## TO A MAN

You seemed a guileless youth enough,
Offering for silk your woven stuff;
But silk was not required by you:
I was the silk you had in view.
With you I crossed the ford, and while
We wandered on for many a mile
I said, "I do not wish delay.
But friends must fix our wedding-day.
Oh, do not let my words give pain,
But with the autumn come again."

And then I used to watch and wait
To see you passing through the gate;
And sometimes when I watched in vain,
My tears would flow like falling rain;
But when I saw my darling boy,
I laughed and cried aloud for joy.
The fortune-tellers, you declared,
Had all pronounced us duly paired;
"Then bring a carriage," I replied,
"And I'll away to be your bride."

## 古今诗选

　　你去占卜问了吉凶啊，全都是吉祥如意的言辞。带着你的车子来吧，好搬运我的嫁妆。

　　桑树的叶子未落的时候啊，枝头都是满目的翠绿。鸣叫的斑鸠啊，可不要贪吃桑葚。年轻的姑娘们啊，不要对男子过于迷恋。男子若是迷恋上姑娘呀，姑娘可以轻易地解脱。若是姑娘迷恋上男子哟，那就很难挣脱了。绿绿的桑叶落了啊，就会变得枯黄。自从我嫁给你以后啊，三年受尽了穷苦煎熬。横流的淇河水啊，浩浩荡荡，淹没了我遭弃后回家的车辆。

　　作为女人啊，我并没有过错，反倒是男人的行为和操行值得思量。随心而为啊没有规矩，三心二意令人心伤。嫁人为妇已三年啦，整天繁重的劳作，无片刻清闲。

　　从来是晚睡早起的劳作啊，辛苦的生活从未改变。待到家业有成以后啊，就渐渐对我施凶暴戾。可怜我的兄弟仍不知我的处境啊，见面时还对我言语讥诮。静下心来细思量啊，只能独处暗自神伤。当年白头偕老的约定啊，回味起来只能使我徒增心伤。浩荡的淇河水啊终有尽头，广阔的湿地啊也会有岸边。还是少年时期的欢乐多啊，大家谈笑起来情意绵绵。当年的海誓山盟啊今犹在耳，哪里想过会是这样的结局。这些事情以后不会再提及，该了结的就让它完全结束吧！

The mulberry-leaf, not yet undone
By autumn chill, shines in the sun.
O tender dove, I would advise,
Beware the fruit that tempts thy eyes!
O maiden fair, not yet a spouse,
List lightly not to lovers' vows!
A man may do this wrong, and time
Will fling its shadow o'er his crime;
A woman who has lost her name
Is doomed to everlasting shame.

The mulberry-tree upon the ground
Now sheds its yellow leaves around.
Three years have slipped away from me,
Since first I shared your poverty;
And now again, alas the day!
Back through the ford I take my way.
My heart is still unchanged, but you
Have uttered words now proved untrue;
And you have left me to deplore
A love that can be mine no more.
For three long years I was your wife,
And led in truth a toilsome life;
Early to rise and late to bed.

古今诗选

Each day alike passed o'er my head.
I honestly fulfilled my part;
And you, — well, you have broke my heart.
The truth my brothers will not know,
So all the more their gibes will flow.
I grieve in silence and repine
That such a wretched fate is mine.

Ah, hand in hand to face old age! —
Instead, I turn a bitter page.
Oh for the river-banks of yore;
Oh for the much-loved marshy shore;
The hours of girlhood, with my hair
Ungathered, as we lingered there.
The words we spoke, that seemed so true,
I little thought that I should rue;
I little thought the vows we swore
Would some day bind us two no more.

古今诗选

# 诗经·蟋蟀(节选)

蟋蟀在堂,岁聿其莫。今我不乐,日月其除。
无已大康,职思其居!好乐无荒,良士瞿瞿。

【今译】

　　蟋蟀进屋避风寒,一年即将要过完。如今再不去行乐,光阴不能再留住。行乐不可没有度,该做事情莫延误。行乐仍不忘正业,君子良士当警悟。

# 击 壤 歌

[先秦] 佚名

日出而作,日入而息,
凿井而饮,耕田而食。
帝力于我何有哉!

【今译】

　　太阳升起就劳作,太阳落山就休息;渴了凿井取水喝,饿了耕田获得食物。帝王的权力和我能有什么关系呢!

## THE CRICKET

The cricket chirrups in the hall,
The year is dying fast;
Now let us hold high festival
Ere the days and months be past.
Yet push not revels to excess
That our fair fame be marred;
Lest pleasures verge to wickedness
Let each be on his guard.

## THE HUSBANDMAN'S SONG

Work, work, — from the rising sun
Till sunset comes and the day is done
I plough the sod
And harrow the clod.
And meat and drink both come to me,
So what care I for the powers that be?

## 尧　戒

[先秦] 佚名

战战栗栗，日谨一日。人莫踬于山，而踬于垤。

【今译】

　　战战栗栗，一天比一天谨慎。人往往不是被大山绊倒，而是被小土堆绊倒。

## 盥　盘　铭

[先秦] 佚名

　　与其溺于人也，宁溺于渊。溺于渊犹可游也，溺于人不可救也。

【今译】

　　与其淹没于小人中，不如淹没于深深的潭水里。淹没于深潭里还可以游出来，淹没于小人之中就不可救治了。

## YAO'S ADVICE

With trembling heart and cautious steps
Walk daily in fear of God.
Though you never trip over a mountain,
You may often trip over a clod.

## INSCRIPTION ON A WASH-BASIN

Oh, rather than sink in the world's foul tide
I would sink in the bottomless main;
For he who sinks in the world's foul tide
In noisome depths shall for ever abide,
But he who sinks in the bottomless main
May hope to float to the surface again.

古今诗选

# 青青河畔草

[汉] 佚名

青青河畔草,郁郁园中柳。
盈盈楼上女,皎皎当窗牖。
娥娥红粉妆,纤纤出素手。
昔为倡家女,今为荡子妇。
荡子行不归,空床难独守。

【今译】

　　青青的草儿长满河边的空地,园子里的柳树显得郁郁葱葱。体态盈盈的女子独自站在楼上,皎洁的月光透过窗户照着她的脸庞。粉妆打扮过的女子容貌非常艳丽,伸出纤纤玉手轻轻地扶着窗子。她曾经是个青楼女子,如今成了游子的妻子。游子在远方游历很久没有回家,而她只能默默地独守空床。

# 涉江采芙蓉

[汉] 佚名

涉江采芙蓉,兰泽多芳草。

## NEGLECTED

Green grows the grass upon the bank,
The willow-shoots are long and lank;
A lady in a glistening gown
Opens the casement and looks down.
The roses on her cheek blush bright,
Her rounded arm is dazzling white;
A singing-girl in early life.
And now a careless roue's wife.
Ah, if he does not mind his own.
He'll find some day the bird has flown!

## PARTED

The red hibiscus and the reed,

采之欲遗谁，所思在远道。
还顾望旧乡，长路漫浩浩。
同心而离居，忧伤以终老。

【今译】

　　跨江去采美丽的荷花，又到沼泽地去摘幽香的兰花。采了花儿要赠给谁呢？送给我日夜思念的远方的爱人。回首遥望故乡的爱人，长路漫漫多么遥远。身处两地的爱人彼此思念，他们心怀忧伤，日渐老去。

# 秋 风 辞

### [西汉] 刘彻

秋风起兮白云飞，草木黄落兮雁南归。
兰有秀兮菊有芳，怀佳人兮不能忘。
泛楼船兮济汾河，横中流兮扬素波。
箫鼓鸣兮发棹歌，欢乐极兮哀情多。
少壮几时兮奈老何！

【今译】

　　秋风刮起啊，白云舞动。草木枯黄啊大雁南归。秀美的是兰花啊，伴着菊花的芳香。我心中思念的佳人啊，怎么能

The fragrant flowers of marsh and mead, —
All these I gather as I stray,
As though for one now far away.
I strive to pierce with straining eyes
The distance that between us lies.
Alas that hearts which beat as one
Should thus be parted and undone!

## AMARI ALIQUID[①]

The autumn blast drives the white scud in the sky,
Leaves fade, and wild geese sweeping south meet the eye;
The scent of late flowers fills the soft air above,
My heart full of thoughts of the lady I love.
In the river the barges for revel-carouse
Are lined by white waves which break over their bows;
Their oarsmen keep time to the piping and drumming.
Yet joy is as naught
Alloyed by the thought

忘。乘坐楼船行驶在汾河上，在河中疾行啊，荡起白色的波浪。吹箫击鼓啊，唱起了船歌，欢乐至极啊，不禁心怀哀伤。年轻的日子太短啊，转眼就要衰老！

# 落叶哀蝉曲

[西汉] 刘彻

罗袂兮无声，玉墀兮尘生。
虚房冷而寂寞，落叶依于重扃。
望彼美之女兮，安得感余心之未宁？

【今译】

　　听不到衣袖挥舞的声音，院子里落满了尘土。没有你的屋子里冷清而又寂寞，飘落的黄叶堆积于宫殿门前。遥望我思念的美人啊，你可知道我心中久久不能平静？

# 怨 歌 行

[西汉] 班婕妤

新裂齐纨素，皎洁如霜雪。

That youth slips away and that old age is coming.

【注】 ①拉丁语。意为"喜欢之人"。

# GONE

The sound of rustling silk is stilled,
With dust the marble courtyard filled;
No footfalls echo on the floor,
Fallen leaves in heaps block up the door...
For she, my pride, my lovely one is lost.
And I am left, in hopeless anguish tossed.

# THE AUTUMN FAN

O fair white silk, fresh from the weaver's loom,

裁作合欢扇，团团似明月。
出入君怀袖，动摇微风发。
常恐秋节至，凉飚夺炎热。
弃捐箧笥中，恩情中道绝。

**【今译】**

　　新做出来的齐地产的丝绢，像霜和雪一般洁白无瑕。把丝绢裁剪成一把合欢圆扇，圆圆的似皎洁的明月。这把扇子伴随在夫君身边，热时轻摇就会凉风袭面。就怕夏季过完秋天到来啊，秋天的凉风会代替夏日的炎热。用不着的团扇被扔进了箱子里，曾经的情义便就此中断。

# 生年不满百

［东汉］佚名

生年不满百，常怀千岁忧。
昼短苦夜长，何不秉烛游！
为乐当及时，何能待来兹。
愚者爱惜费，但为后世嗤。
仙人王子乔，难可与等期。

Clear as the frost, bright as the winter snow —
See! friendship fashions out of thee a fan.
Round as the round moon shines in heaven above;
At home, abroad, a close companion thou,
Stirring at every move the grateful gale;
And yet I fear, ah me! that autumn chills,
Cooling the dying summer's torrid rage,
Will see thee laid neglected on the shelf.
All thought of by gone days, like them by-gone.

## CARPE DIEM

Man reaches scarce a hundred, yet his tears
Would fill a lifetime of a thousand years.
When days are short and night's long hours move slow,
Why not with lamp in search of pleasure go?
This day alone gives sure enjoyment — this!
Why then await tomorrow's doubtful bliss?
Fools grudge to spend their wealth while life abides,

## 【今译】

　　人的一生尚不满百年,但却常常怀有千年的感叹和忧愁。白昼太短而长夜漫漫,为什么不端着烛火在夜里畅游呢?人生啊就应该及时行乐,怎能总是期待来年呢?愚蠢的人啊总是吝啬守财,却往往为后人所嗤笑。像王子乔那样成为神仙,这样的事情我们很难去期待。

# 驱车上东门

### [东汉] 佚名

驱车上东门,遥望郭北墓。白杨何萧萧,松柏夹广路。
下有陈死人,杳杳即长暮。潜寐黄泉下,千载永不寤。
浩浩阴阳移,年命如朝露。人生忽如寄,寿无金石固。
万岁更相送,贤圣莫能度。服食求神仙,多为药所误。
不如饮美酒,被服纨与素。

## 【今译】

　　驾车来到洛阳城的东门,遥望城北那一片墓地。墓前的白杨发出萧萧声,大路两边种满了常青的松柏。地下埋着早已逝去的人,犹如堕入永恒的漫漫长夜。默默长眠于黄泉下,千年万年再也不会醒来。岁月流转如江河东去,生命之短如清晨朝露。人人匆匆就像寄居的过客,寿命没法像金石那样

And then posterity their thrift derides.
We cannot hope, like Wang Tzu-ch'iao, to rise
And find a paradise beyond the skies.




# THE ELIXIR OF LIFE


Forth from the eastern gate my steeds I drive,
And lo! a cemetery meets my view;
Aspens around in wild luxuriance thrive,
The road is fringed with fir and pine and yew.
Beneath my feet lie the forgotten dead.
Wrapped in a twilight of eternal gloom;
Down by the Yellow Springs their earthy bed,
And everlasting silence is their doom.
How fast the lights and shadows come and go!
Like morning dew our fleeting life has passed;
Man, a poor traveller on earth below,
Is gone, while brass and stone can still outlast.

长久。自古都是生死更迭轮转，圣贤之人也无法超脱。至于服丹药想成神成仙，往往被丹药欺骗和耽误。还不如时常喝点美酒，穿着绸锦及时享乐呢。

# 杂　诗

### ［东汉］孔融

远送新行客，岁暮乃来归。
入门望爱子，妻妾向人悲。
闻子不可见，日已潜光辉。
孤坟在西北，常念君来迟。
褰裳上墟丘，但见蒿与薇。
白骨归黄泉，肌体乘尘飞。
生时不识父，死后知我谁。
孤魂游穷暮，飘摇安所依。
人生图嗣息，尔死我念追。
俯仰内伤心，不觉泪沾衣。
人生自有命，但恨生日希。

Time is inexorable, and in vain
Against his might the holiest mortal strives;
Can we then hope this precious boon to gain,
By strange elixirs to prolong our lives?...
Oh, rather quaff good liquor while we may,
And dress in silk and satin every day!


# A FIRST-BORN


The wanderer reaches home with joy
From absence of a year and more;
His eye seeks a beloved boy —
His wife lies weeping on the floor.

They whisper he is gone. The glooms
Of evening fall; beyond the gate
A lonely grave in outline looms
To greet the sire who came too late.
Forth to the little mound he flings,
Where wild-flowers bloom on every side...
His bones are in the Yellow Springs,

古今诗选

**【今译】**

　　远道送走一位新交的朋友后，直到年底才赶回家里。进了门急着想见到心爱的儿子，却见妻妾正悲伤地哭泣。听说心爱的儿子已死，再也见不到了，太阳似乎也失去了光芒。妻妾说，儿子的坟墓孤独地立在西北方，他生前常念叨父亲，为什么还不回来。提起衣服的下摆走到坟丘边，只见坟上已长满了蓬蒿与野豌豆。黄泉下埋着儿子的白骨，曾经鲜活的肌体早已化作尘埃飞散。儿子活着的时候年龄太小尚不认识父亲，死了以后又怎么知道我是谁。儿子的孤魂在地下无尽的黑暗里游走，飘飘摇摇哪里才是他的依靠？人都希望能有子嗣传递生命，儿子一死，留给我的是无穷无尽的追忆。抬头看天，俯身看地，无限伤心，不觉间泪水已沾湿了衣裳。虽然人生在世生死有命，只是恨上天给我儿子的寿命太短了。

# 室　　思（其三）

[东汉] 徐干

浮云何洋洋，愿因通我辞。
飘摇不可寄，徙倚徒相思。
人离皆复会，君独无返期。
自君之出矣，明镜暗不治。
思君如流水，何有穷已时。

His flesh like dust is scattered wide.
"O child who never knew thy sire,
For ever now to be unknown,
Ere long thy wandering ghost shall tire
Of flitting friendless and alone.

"O son, man's greatest earthly boon,
With thee I bury hopes and fears."
He bowed his head in grief and soon
His breast was wet with rolling tears.
Life's dread uncertainty he knows,
But oh for this untimely close!

## AN ABSENT HUSBAND

O floating clouds that swim in heaven above
Bear on your wings these words to him I love...
Alas, you float along nor heed my pain,
And leave me here to love and long in vain!
I see other dear ones to their homes return,

## 【今译】

　　浮云在天上飘来飘去、舒卷自如，我想委托它给远在异乡的丈夫捎几句话。可是浮云飘摇，变幻莫测，实在不可寄托，我徘徊犹豫，徒增相思，更加烦恼罢了。别的夫妻别离后终究还能团聚，唯独你走后就一直没有归期。自从你离开家以后啊，明亮的镜子落满灰尘也懒得擦拭。对你的思念犹如那连绵不绝的流水，真不知道何时才是个尽头。

# 短　歌　行

### ［三国］曹丕

仰瞻帷幕，俯察几筵。其物为故，其人不存。
神灵倏忽，弃我遐迁。靡瞻靡恃，泣涕连连。
呦呦游鹿，衔草鸣麑。翩翩飞鸟，挟子巢栖。
我独孤茕，怀此百离。忧心孔疚，莫我能知。
人亦有言，忧令人老。嗟我白发，生一何蚤。
长吟永叹，怀我圣考。曰仁者寿，胡不是保。

## 【今译】

　　抬头瞻仰灵堂上的帷幕，俯首细看几案上的灵位。物品还是过去的样子，而我的亲人却已不在人世。亲人的魂灵突然走了，就这样把我遗弃，永远走了。从此无依无靠再也见

And for his coming shall not I too yearn?
Since my lord left — ah me, unhappy day! —
My mirror's dust has not been brushed away;
My heart, like running water, knows no peace,
But bleeds and bleeds forever without cease.

# ON THE DEATH OF HIS FATHER

I look up, the curtains are there as of yore;
I look down, and there is the mat on the floor,
These things I behold, but the man is no more.
To the infinite azure his spirit has flown,
And I am left friendless, uncared-for, alone,
Of solace bereft, save to weep and to moan.
The deer on the hillside caressingly bleat.
And offer the grass for their young ones to eat,
While birds of the air to their nestlings bring meat.

But I a poor orphan must ever remain,

不到亲人面,不由得我眼泪涟涟。奔走的母鹿声声呼唤,衔来青草把小鹿喂养。天空的鸟儿在盘旋,是要带着小鸟飞回巢。唯独我孤苦伶仃,心中充满失去亲人的痛楚。我内心的痛苦啊,没人能真正体会。古人说,过度忧伤会使人衰老。可叹我的白发啊,早早就已长满!长歌伴着长叹,深深地把父亲怀念。古语说,有仁德的人可以长寿,可为什么我的父亲不能长寿百年?

# 七 步 诗

[三国] 曹植

煮豆持作羹,漉菽以为汁。
萁在釜下燃,豆在釜中泣。
本自同根生,相煎何太急?

【今译】

　　煮豆用来做豆羹,把豆子的残渣过滤后留下豆汁。豆秆在锅底燃烧,锅里的豆子在哭泣。豆子和豆秆本是从同一条根上长出来的,豆秆怎能这样急迫地煎熬豆子呢?

My heart, still so young, overburdened with pain
For him I shall never set eyes on again.
'Tis a well-worn old saying, which all men allow,
That grief stamps the deepest of lines on the brow:
Alas for my hair, it is silvery now!
Alas for my father, cut off in his pride!
Alas that no more I may stand by his side!
Oh where were the gods when that great hero died?

## THE BROTHERS

A fine dish of beans had been placed in the pot
With a view to a good mess of pottage, all hot.
The beanstalks, aflame, a fierce heat were begetting,
The beans in the pot were all fuming and fretting.
Yet the beans and the stalks were not born to be foes;
Oh why should these hurry to finish off those?

# 吴 楚 歌

[西晋] 傅玄

燕人美兮赵女佳,其室则迩兮限层崖。
云为车兮风为马,玉在山兮兰在野。
云无期兮风有止,思多端兮谁能理?

【今译】

　　燕女漂亮啊赵女佳,居所近在咫尺啊,却如隔了层层山崖。把云当车、把风作马啊,去找寻她。她隐居山野、如兰似玉啊。云有时看不见啊,风有时会停,我对美人无尽的仰慕之情啊,又有谁能帮我排解。

# 车遥遥篇

[西晋] 傅玄

车遥遥兮马洋洋,追思君兮不可忘。
君安游兮西入秦,愿为影兮随君身。
君在阴兮影不见,君依光兮妾所愿!

## LOVERS PARTED

In the Kingdom of Yen, a young gallant resides,
In the Kingdom of Chao, a fair damsel abides;
No long leagues of wearisome road intervene,
But a chain of steep mountains is set in between.
Ye clouds, on your broad bosoms bear me afar,
The winds for my horses made fast to my car!
Ah, jade lies deep hid in the bowels of earth;
To the fair epidendrum, the prairie gives birth;
And the clouds in the sky, they come not at call;
And the fickle breeze rises, alas, but to fall.
And so I am left with my thoughts to repine,
And think of that loved one who ne'er can be mine.

## AFTER PARTING

Thy chariot and horses
have gone, and I fret
And long for the lover

**【今译】**

　　车子已走向远方啊马儿飞驰,我的思念追随您啊永不能忘。您怀揣梦想啊西入秦地,我愿像影子一样啊伴随您身旁。您在暗处啊看不见影子,我愿您永远依傍着光亮。

# 拟　　古(其四)

[东晋] 陶渊明

迢迢百尺楼,分明望四荒,
暮作归云宅,朝为飞鸟堂。
山河满目中,平原独茫茫。
古时功名士,慷慨争此场。
一旦百岁后,相与还北邙。
松柏为人伐,高坟互低昂。
颓基无遗主,游魂在何方!
荣华诚足贵,亦复可怜伤。

I ne'er can forget.
O wanderer, bound
in far countries to dwell,
Would I were thy shadow! —
I'd follow thee well.
And though clouds and though darkness
My presence should hide,
In the bright light of day
I would stand by thy side!

# SIC TRANSIT

A tower a hundred feet erect
Looks round upon the scene which girds;
'Tis here at eve the clouds collect,
At dawn a trysting-place for birds.
Here hills and streams the observer hold,
Or boundless prairie mocks the eyes:
Some famous warriors of old
Made this their bloody battle-prize.
The centuries of time roll on,

**【今译】**

　　我站在高高的百尺楼上，目及四方，荒远而清晰可见。晚上白云把它当作家园，白天飞鸟集聚把它当作厅堂。远处的大好河山皆入目，近处的平地一片辽阔。过去建功立业者，曾奋力角逐在此场。一旦离开人世了，最终结局都要葬于北邙。坟墓旁的松柏终被砍伐，坟堆高低起伏有些凄凉。无主的坟墓已坍塌毁坏，谁知道孤魂流落在何方！生前荣华虽可贵，结局都是凄凉而悲伤！

# 拟　　古(其五)

[东晋] 陶渊明

东方有一士，被服常不完；
三旬九遇食，十年著一冠。
辛勤无此比，常有好容颜。
我欲观其人，晨去越河关。
青松夹路生，白云宿檐端。
知我故来意，取琴为我弹。
上弦惊别鹤，下弦操孤鸾。
愿留就君住，从令至岁寒。

And I, a traveller, passing there,
Mark firs and cypresses all gone.
And grave-mounds, high and low, laid bare.
The ruined tombs uncared-for stand —
Where do their wandering spirits hide? —
Oh, glory makes us great and grand,
And yet it has its seamy side.

## A RECLUSE

A scholar lives on yonder hill,
His clothes are rarely whole to view,
Nine times a month he eats his fill.
Once in ten years his hat is new.
A wretched lot! — and yet the while
He ever wears a sunny smile.
Longing to know what like was he,
At dawn my steps a path unclosed
Where dark firs left the passage free
And on the eaves the white clouds dozed.

【今译】

　　东方有位隐士，身上衣衫褴褛。一月吃饭九次，帽子戴了十年。辛劳无人能比，整日满面笑容。我想前去拜访，清晨渡河越关。路旁两行青松，屋檐白云缭绕。听到我的来意，为我弹奏乐曲。先为我弹《别鹤》，又为我弹《孤鸾》。我愿长陪您住，直到岁尽暮寒。

# 读《山海经》(其五)

[东晋] 陶渊明

翩翩三青鸟，毛色奇可怜。
朝为王母使，暮归三危山。
我欲因此鸟，具向王母言：
在世无所须，惟酒与长年。

【今译】

　　翩翩飞舞的三青鸟，美丽羽毛甚好看。清早去为王母使，晚归居处三危山。我想拜托三青鸟，去向王母表衷言。在世此生无所求，但愿长寿和美酒。

But he, as spying my intent,
Seized his guitar and swept the strings;
Up flew a crane towards heaven bent,
And now a startled pheasant springs...
Oh, let me rest with thee until
The winter winds again blow chill!

# A PRAYER

Ye fluttering birds in plumage gay
That to and fro direct your flight, —
The Western Mother's court by day,
The far-off mountain-peaks at night, —
Oh, be my messengers and go
And bear to her these words of mine:
I ask for nothing here below
Save length of years and depth of wine!

## 拟行路难(其三)

[南朝宋] 鲍照

璇闺玉墀上椒阁,文窗绣户垂罗幕。
中有一人字金兰,被服纤罗采芳藿。
春燕差池风散梅,开帏对景弄禽爵。
含歌揽涕恒抱愁,人生几时得为乐。
宁作野中之双凫,不愿云间之别鹤。

【今译】

　　踏着美玉铺就的台阶来到椒房,罗绮做成的帷幕垂在雕花的窗边。屋里有个女子名字叫金兰,她身上穿着细罗衣裳,散发着芬芳。春燕在被风吹落的梅花间飞来飞去,她掀起帷帐迎着阳光独自饮酒自赏。她欲歌还休,眼中含泪,满心忧伤,哀叹人生的快乐到底在何时何方。宁愿做贫贱野地里一对野鸭子,也不做高翔于云彩间的独鹤。

## 赠逸民诗(其十一)

[南朝梁] 萧衍

如垄生木,木有异心。
如林鸣鸟,鸟有殊音。

## ALONE

What do these halls of jasper mean, and shining floor,
Where tapestries of satin screen window and door?
A lady on a lonely seat, embroidering
Fair flowers which seem to smell as sweet
                as buds in spring.
Swallows flit past, a zephyr shakes
                the plum-blooms down—,
She draws the blind, a goblet takes
                her thoughts to drown;
And now she sits in tears, or hums, nursing her grief
That in her life joy rarely comes to bring relief...
Oh for the humble turtle's flight, my mate and I;
Not the lone crane far out of sight beyond the sky!

## ULTIMATE CAUSES

Trees grow, not alike, by the mound and the moat;
Birds sing in the forest with varying note;

如江游鱼，鱼有浮沉。
岩岩山高，湛湛水深。
事迹易见，理相难寻。

**【今译】**

如同高大的树木，树心位置必有不同。如同树林中的鸟儿，鸣叫的声音也各不一样。如同江河中的鱼儿，游起来有浅有深。巍峨的高山多么伟岸，幽深的水不可测知。虽然这些都能轻易见到，但是其中的本质规律却难以探究。

# 效阮公诗(其十)

[南朝梁] 江淹

少年学击剑，从师至幽州。
燕赵兵马地，唯见古时丘。
登城望山水，平原独悠悠。
寒暑有往来，功名安可留。

**【今译】**

年少时学习剑术，来到幽州城。这里曾是燕赵对峙的战场，此时遗留下的只有古丘。登上幽州城楼远眺，远处平原开阔。寒暑时光流逝，带走的还有战士的功名。

Of the fish in the river some dive and some float.
The mountains rise high and the waters sink low.
But the why and the wherefore we never can know.

# FORGOTTEN

To learn the art of fencing, forth
I wandered, with my master, north.
I saw an ancient battle-plain
Engirt by hills which still remain;
And while I gazed upon the scene,
A wide expanse of sky and green,
I thought how like a summer's day
Each warrior's name has passed away.

## 人日思归（节选）

[隋] 薛道衡

入春才七日，离家已二年。
人归落雁后，思发在花前。

【今译】

入春才刚刚过了七天，离开家已经两年。回家的日子要落在春回大地北飞的雁群之后了，但是想回家的念头却在春花开放以前就有了。

## 野　　望

[唐] 王绩

东皋薄暮望，徙倚欲何依？
树树皆秋色，山山唯落晖。
牧人驱犊返，猎马带禽归。
相顾无相识，长歌怀采薇。

【今译】

傍晚在东皋村极目远眺，徘徊彷徨不知该身归何方。田野里的树林都染上秋天的色彩，远处的山峰都覆盖着落日的

## ANTICIPATION

A week in the spring
                to the exile appears,
Like an absence from home of
                a couple of years.
If home, with the wild geese of autumn,
                we're going,
Our hearts will be off ere the spring flowers
                are blowing.

## IN ABSENCE

At eve, I stand upon the bank and gaze;
Restless, I know not where my bark may rest;
I see the forest through the autumn haze;
I see the hills of radiance all divest;
I see the herdsman homing o'er the lea;
I see the huntsman's laden horse return...
Alas, no loved one comes to beckon me! —

古今诗选

余晖。牧人驱赶着小牛回到了家里,猎人骑着马带着猎物疾驰而归。这些人没有一个是我曾经相识的,让人哀伤苦闷,只有长啸高歌《采薇》的诗句。

## 滕王阁诗

[唐] 王勃

滕王高阁临江渚,佩玉鸣鸾罢歌舞。
画栋朝飞南浦云,珠帘暮卷西山雨。
闲云潭影日悠悠,物换星移几度秋。
阁中帝子今安在?槛外长江空自流!

【今译】

  巍然高耸的滕王阁俯临着江心的沙洲,歌舞停后佩玉鸾铃寂静无声。早晨南浦飞来的轻云掠过画栋,傍晚西山飘来的烟雨卷入珠帘。映入江中白云的影子悠然漂浮,时光流逝,不知已过了多少个春秋。修建这座楼阁的滕王如今在何处?空余那栏杆外滔滔的江水径自东流。

I sit and croon the thoughts that in me burn.

# ICHABOD

Near these islands a palace was built by a prince,
But its music and song have departed long since;
The hill-mists of morning sweep down on the halls,
At night the red curtains lie furled on the walls.
The clouds o'er the water their shadows still cast.
Things change like the stars: how few
                        autumns have passed
And yet where is that prince? Where is he? —
No reply,
Save the plash of the stream rolling ceaselessly by.

## 登幽州台歌

〔唐〕陈子昂

前不见古人,后不见来者。
念天地之悠悠,独怆然而涕下。

【今译】

　　往前看不见古代招贤的圣主,向后看不见后世纳士的明君。想到那天地苍茫无穷无尽,不由得心怀感伤而热泪纷纷。

## 感遇(其十九)

〔唐〕陈子昂

圣人不利己,忧济在元元。
黄屋非尧意,瑶台安可论。
吾闻西方化,清净道弥敦。
奈何穷金玉,雕刻以为尊。
云构山林尽,瑶图珠翠烦。
鬼工尚未可,人力安能存。
夸愚适增累,矜智道逾昏。

## REGRETS

My eyes saw not the men of old;
And now their age away has rolled
I weep — to think I shall not see
The heroes of posterity!

## AGAINST IDOLS

On Self the Prophet never rests his eye,
His to relieve the doom of humankind;
No fairy palaces beyond the sky,
Rewards to come, are present to his mind.
And I have heard the faith by Buddha taught
Lauded as pure and free from earthly taint;
Why then these carved and graven idols, fraught
With gold and silver, gems, and jade, and paint?

【今译】

　　圣贤都是无私为民的,所忧虑的都是黎民百姓。尧从不向往豪华的车舆,更不用提奢侈的宫殿。我听说西方佛教提倡:教中之人应清净淳朴。又怎能耗尽黄金美玉,用来建造神圣的庙宇。为建寺庙而伐尽山林,为精美装饰而搜尽珠宝。如此工程鬼神尚难建造,仅凭人力又怎能实现。如此排场太劳民伤财,看似聪明而实则愚蠢。

# 回乡偶书

[唐] 贺知章

少小离家老大回,乡音无改鬓毛衰。
儿童相见不相识,笑问客从何处来。

【今译】

　　少年时离开家乡,到老了才回来,口音虽没变化,却已是双鬓斑白。生活在家乡的儿童没有见过我,笑嘻嘻地问,客人是从哪里来呀?

The heavens that roof this earth, mountain and dale,
All that is great and grand shall pass away;
And if the art of gods may not prevail,
Shall man's poor handiwork escape decay?
Fools that ye are! In this ignoble light
The true faith fades and passes out of sight.

## THE RETURN

Bowed down with age I seek my native place,
Unchanged my speech, my hair is silvered now;
My very children do not know my face,
But smiling ask, "O stranger, whence art thou?"

古今诗选

## 和赵员外桂阳桥遇佳人

[唐] 宋之问

江雨朝飞浥细尘,阳桥花柳不胜春。
金鞍白马来从赵,玉面红妆本姓秦。
妒女犹怜镜中发,侍儿堪感路傍人。
荡舟为乐非吾事,自叹空闺梦寐频。

【今译】

　　清晨的一阵江雨把空气洗得清新明丽,阳桥一带桃红柳绿,一派春光盎然。骑着金鞍白马的是从赵家来的员外,容颜洁白红妆艳丽的佳人姓秦。如此佳人让嫉妒心强的女子也心生怜爱而感叹容颜易逝,侍从见了佳人也感觉不到旁人的存在,被佳人所吸引。心中思念佳人,荡舟游春的赵员外忘记他来此的初衷了,思念郎君的佳人独守空房,经常梦见倾心的赵郎。

## 望月怀远

[唐] 张九龄

海上生明月,天涯共此时。
情人怨遥夜,竟夕起相思。

## A VISION

The dust of the morn had been laid by a shower,
And the trees by the bridge were all covered
                              with flower,
When a white palfrey passed with a saddle of gold,
And a damsel as fair as the fairest of old.
But she veiled so discreetly her charms from my eyes
That the boy who was with her quite felt for my sighs;
And although not a light-o'-love reckoned, I deem,
It was hard that this vision should pass like a dream.

## BY MOONLIGHT

Over the sea the round moon rises bright,
And floods the horizon with its silver light.

灭烛怜光满，披衣觉露滋。
不堪盈手赠，还寝梦佳期。

【今译】

　　一轮明月从海上升起，照着天各一方的你我。有情人都抱怨长夜漫漫，彼此思念彻夜难眠。吹灭蜡烛，月光洒满屋子，夜半的露水打湿了身上披着的外衣。虽不能把皎洁的月光双手捧给你，但我仍可以尽快入梦共度相见的佳期。

# 宿业师山房待丁大不至

[唐] 孟浩然

夕阳度西岭，群壑倏已暝。
松月生夜凉，风泉满清听。
樵人归欲尽，烟鸟栖初定。
之子期宿来，孤琴候萝径。

【今译】

　　夕阳已落入西边的山岭，群山万壑骤然显得昏暗幽暝。月光透过松林平添夜晚的凉意，风声和着泉水声发出清脆的声响。打柴的樵夫们都要回家去了，雾霭中的归鸟也落巢栖定。本来和你约好今晚来这里住宿，我独自抱琴站在路上等你。

In absence lovers grieve that nights should be,
But all the livelong night I think of thee.
I blow my lamp out to enjoy this rest,
And shake the gathering dewdrop from my vest.
Alas! I cannot share with thee these beams,
So lay me down to seek thee in my dreams.

# WAITING

The sun has sunk behind the western hill,
And darkness glides across the vale below;
Between the firs the moon shines cold and chill,
No breezes whisper to the streamlet's flow.
Belated woodsmen homeward hurry past,
Birds seek their evening refuge in the tree:
O my beloved, wilt thou come at last?
With lute, among the flowers, I wait for thee.

古今诗选

# 夏日南亭怀辛大

[唐] 孟浩然

山光忽西落,池月渐东上。
散发乘夜凉,开轩卧闲敞。
荷风送香气,竹露滴清响。
欲取鸣琴弹,恨无知音赏。
感此怀故人,终霄劳梦想。

【今译】

　　西山的夕阳忽然沉了下去,池塘边的月亮慢慢从东方升起。披散开头发正好在夜间乘凉,打开窗户躺在幽静宽敞的地方。晚风吹过荷花带来阵阵清香,竹叶上滴下的露水发出清脆的声响。很想取琴来弹奏一曲,可惜没有知音来此欣赏。感叹中我又思念起老朋友,只愿整夜都在梦里与他叙谈。

# 宿建德江

[唐] 孟浩然

移舟泊烟渚,日暮客愁新。
野旷天低树,江清月近人。

## IN DREAMLAND

The sun has set behind the western slope,
The eastern moon lies mirrored in the pool;
With streaming hair my balcony I ope,
And stretch my limbs out to enjoy the cool.
Loaded with lotus-scent the breeze sweeps by,
Clear dripping drops from tall bamboos I hear,
I gaze upon my idle lute and sigh:
Alas no sympathetic soul is near!
And so I doze, the while before mine eyes
Dear friends of other days in dream-clad forms arise.

## AT ANCHOR

I steer my boat to anchor
    by the mist-clad river eyot,
And mourn the dying day that brings me

古今诗选

【今译】

  我把小船停泊在烟雾缭绕的沙洲,周围暮色苍茫让游子平添几分新愁。空旷的原野使得天际线比树木还低,清澈的江水映着明月显得离游子很近很近。

# 罢相作

## [唐] 李适之

避贤初罢相,乐圣且衔杯。
为问门前客,今朝几个来。

【今译】

  为了让贤我辞掉了宰相的职务,今后就可以天天举杯欢饮美酒了。就想问问昔日络绎不绝登门的宾客,到了今天还有几人肯来找我?

     nearer to my fate.
  Across the woodland wild I see
      the sky lean on the trees,
While close to hand the mirrored moon
      floats on the shining seas.

## OUT OF OFFICE

For my betters — my office resigned —
     I make way,
And seek with the wine-cup to shorten the day.
You ask for the friends who once thronged in my hall:
Alas! with my place they have gone, one and all.

## 竹 里 馆

[唐] 王维

独坐幽篁里,弹琴复长啸。
深林人不知,明月来相照。

【今译】

　　独自坐在幽深的竹林里,时而弹弹琴,时而仰天长啸。没人知道我在这僻静的竹林深处,只有一轮皎洁的明月陪伴着我。

## 山中送别

[唐] 王维

山中相送罢,日暮掩柴扉。
春草年年绿,王孙归不归。

【今译】

　　在山中刚把客人送走,傍晚的太阳照着关闭的柴门。青草每年都会有再度绿的时候,在外漂泊的游子何时才能归来。

## OVERLOOKED

Beneath the bamboo grove, alone,
I seize my lute and sit and croon;
No ear to hear me, save mine own;
No eye to see me, save the moon.

## GOODBYE

We parted at the gorge and cried "Good cheer!"
The sun was setting as I closed my door;
Methought, the spring will come again next year,
But he may come no more.

## 杂　诗

[唐] 王维

君自故乡来，应知故乡事。
来日绮窗前，寒梅著花未？

【今译】

　　您从家乡来到这里，理应知道家乡的事。来的那天花窗前面，梅花是否已经绽开？

## 送　别

[唐] 王维

下马饮君酒，问君何所之。
君言不得意，归卧南山陲。
但去莫复问，白云无尽时。

【今译】

　　朋友啊，下马来饮一杯酒吧，请问您要去哪里呀？您说现在郁郁不得志，想要归隐在终南山旁。您只管去吧，我不会再问，且看那天边无尽的白云在空中飘浮。

## A RENCONTRE

Sir, from my dear old home you come,
And all its glories you can name;
Oh tell me, — has the winter-plum
Yet blossomed o'er the window-frame?

## GOODBYE TO MENG HAO-JAN

Dismounted, o'er wine we had said our last say;
Then I whisper, "Dear friend, tell me whither away."
"Alas!" he replied, "I am sick of life's ills
"And I long for repose on the slumbering hills.
"But oh seek not to pierce where my footsteps
                                          may stray:
"The white clouds will soothe me for ever and ay."

## 黄 鹤 楼

[唐] 崔颢

昔人已乘黄鹤去,此地空余黄鹤楼。
黄鹤一去不复返,白云千载空悠悠。
晴川历历汉阳树,芳草萋萋鹦鹉洲。
日暮乡关何处是?烟波江上使人愁。

【今译】

  传说中的仙人早已骑着黄鹤而去,这里只留下空荡荡的黄鹤楼。仙人骑着黄鹤走后就再也没有回来,只有天上的白云来来回回飘荡不息。远眺晴川阁的绿树历历在目,鹦鹉洲的芳草更是显得郁郁葱葱。那黄昏时分的故乡在哪里呀,面对烟波渺渺的大江令人发愁!

## 咏 萤 火

[唐] 李白

雨打灯难灭,风吹色更明。
若非天上去,定作月边星。

## HOME LONGINGS

Here a mortal once sailed up to heaven on a crane,
And the Yellow-Crane Kiosque will for ever remain;
But the bird flew away and will come back no more,
Though the white clouds are there as the
                    white clouds of yore.

Away to the east lie fair forests of trees,
From the flowers on the west comes
                    a scent-laden breeze,
Yet my eyes daily turn to their far-away home,
Beyond the broad River, its waves, and its foam.

## TO A FIREFLY

Rain cannot quench thy lantern's light,
Wind makes it shine more brightly bright;
Oh why not fly to heaven afar,
And twinkle near the moon — a star?

【今译】

雨水打在灯光上灯不灭,风吹过灯光时灯光更明。假若不是要到天上去,那也一定是月亮旁的一颗星。

# 江夏别宋之悌

[唐] 李白

楚水清若空,遥将碧海通。
人分千里外,兴在一杯中。
谷鸟吟晴日,江猿啸晚风。
平生不下泪,于此泣无穷。

【今译】

楚水清澈得似乎空无,却与遥远的大海相连。我们将要远别于千里之外,心里话都在手捧的一杯酒中。天晴时山间的鸟儿不停鸣叫,江岸的猿猴却在晚风中啼号。我这一生还没有掉过流泪,此时此刻却是泪流不止。

## AT PARTING

The river rolls crystal as clear as the sky,
To blend far away with the blue waves of ocean;
Man alone, when the hour of departure is nigh,
With the wine cup can soothe his emotion.
The birds of the valley sing loud in the sun,
Where the gibbons their vigils will shortly be keeping;
I thought that with tears I had long ago done,
But now I shall never cease weeping.

# 静 夜 思

［唐］李白

床前明月光，疑是地上霜。
举头望明月，低头思故乡。

【今译】

　　明亮的月光照在床前，我还以为是起了秋霜。抬起头凝视这一轮明月，低下头来又想起了我的故乡。

# 独坐敬亭山

［唐］李白

众鸟高飞尽，孤云独去闲。
相看两不厌，只有敬亭山。

【今译】

　　群鸟越飞越高已经了无踪迹，天上一片孤云独自飘来飘去。和我彼此对视而互不生厌的，只有眼前这座沉默不语的敬亭山。

## NIGHT THOUGHTS

I wake, and moonbeams play around my bed,
Glittering like hoar-frost to my wondering eyes;
Up towards the glorious moon I raise my head,
Then lay me down, — and thoughts of home arise.

## COMPANIONS

The birds have all flown to their roost in the tree,
The last cloud has just floated lazily by;
But we never tire of each other, not we.
As we sit there together, — the mountains and I.

## 秋　思

[唐] 李白

燕支黄叶落，妾望自登台。
海上碧云断，单于秋色来。
胡兵沙塞合，汉使玉关回。
征客无归日，空悲蕙草摧。

【今译】

　　燕支山上枯黄的树叶随风飘落，女子登上高台，独自眺望。碧空中的云彩被风吹得纷纷散去，在萧瑟的秋风中匈奴单于带兵打了过来。匈奴军队已经在沙漠中的要塞集结完毕，汉使因交通阻断被迫在玉门关折回。出征在外的亲人一直没有归期，女子像蕙草渐渐枯萎一样黯然伤悲。

## 乌　夜　啼

[唐] 李白

黄云城边乌欲栖，归飞哑哑枝上啼。
机中织锦秦川女，碧纱如烟隔窗语。
停梭怅然忆远人，独宿孤房泪如雨。

## FROM A BELVIDERE

With yellow leaves the hill is strown,
A young wife gazes o'er the scene,
The sky with grey clouds overthrown,
While autumn swoops upon the green.

See, Tartar troops mass on the plain;
Homeward our envoy hurries on;
When will her lord come back again? ...
To find her youth and beauty gone!

## FOR HER HUSBAND

Homeward, at dusk, the clanging rookery
                    wings its eager flight;
Then, chattering on the branches, all

【今译】

  黄云城边的乌鸦即将归巢歇息了,飞回来的时候盘旋在树枝上面哑哑啼叫。正在织机前织布的秦川女子,隔着如烟的绿色窗纱喃喃自语。她停下织梭怅然思念远方的丈夫,想到自己独守空房不由得泪如雨下。

# 春日醉起言志

[唐] 李白

处世若大梦,胡为劳其生?
所以终日醉,颓然卧前楹。
觉来眄庭前,一鸟花间鸣。
借问此何时?春风语流莺。
感之欲叹息,对酒还自倾。
浩歌待明月,曲尽已忘情。

【今译】

  人生在世好像一场大梦,为什么还要辛劳终生呢?所以

      are pairing for the night.
Plying her busy loom, a high-born
      dame is sitting near,
And through the silken window-screen
      their voices strike her ear.
She stops, and thinks of the absent spouse
      she may never see again;
And late in the lonely hours of night
      her tears flow down like rain.

## "THE BEST OF LIFE IS BUT..."

What is life after all but a dream?
And why should such pother be made?

Better far to be tipsy, I deem,
And doze all day long in the shade.

When I wake and look out on the lawn,
I hear midst the flowers a bird sing;
I ask, "Is it evening or dawn?"

> 古今诗选

应该整天沉醉在酒里,醉倒就随意躺在前庭。酒醒后睡眼蒙眬向庭院看去,一只鸟儿正在花丛中鸣啼。请问现在是什么时候啊?春风只和流莺声声低语。对此我真想大发感慨,但还是端起酒杯自斟自饮。我想长啸高歌邀请天上的明月,可酒罢曲终又让我沉醉忘怀。

# 金陵酒肆留别

[唐] 李白

风吹柳花满店香,吴姬压酒唤客尝。
金陵子弟来相送,欲行不行各尽觞。
请君试问东流水,别意与之谁短长。

【今译】

春风吹起柳絮,店里飘满酒香,吴女取出美酒邀请客人来品尝。金陵的朋友们出来给我送行,欲走还留之际大家一饮而尽把酒杯高举。请您问问这向东奔流的江水啊,朋友们离别的情意与它比谁短谁长?

The mango-bird whistles, "'Tis spring."
Overpower'd with the beautiful sight,
Another full goblet I pour,
And would sing till the moon rises bright —
But soon I'm as drunk as before.


## FAREWELL BY THE RIVER


The breeze blows the willow-scent in from
                                        the dell,
While Phyllis with bumpers would fain
                                        cheer us up;
Dear friends press around me to bid me
                                        farewell:
Goodbye! and goodbye! — and yet just
                                        one more cup...
I whisper, Thou'lt see this great stream flow away
Ere I cease to love as I love thee today!

## 送孟浩然之广陵

[唐] 李白

故人西辞黄鹤楼,烟花三月下扬州。
孤帆远影碧空尽,唯见长江天际流。

【今译】

　　我的老朋友向西辞别了黄鹤楼,在百花盛开的春天里要去扬州。一叶孤舟逐渐消失在水天尽头,眼前只剩下滔滔江水向天际奔流!

## 秋　风　词

[唐] 李白

秋风清,秋月明。落叶聚还散,寒鸦栖复惊。
相思相见知何日,此时此夜难为情。

【今译】

　　秋风如此清凉,秋月如此明亮。枯黄的落叶被风刮得聚拢又散开,连栖息在树上的寒鸦都被惊飞。我们彼此相思何时才能相见啊,在这秋夜时分让人感到别离情深。

## GONE

At the Yellow-Crane pagoda, where we
               stopped to bid adieu,
The mists and flowers of April seemed
               to wish good speed to you.
At the Emerald Isle, your lessening sail had
               vanished from my eye,
And left me with the River, rolling onward
               to the sky.

## NO INSPIRATION

The autumn breeze is blowing,
The autumn moon is glowing,
The falling leaves collect but to disperse.
The parson-crow flies here and there
               with ever restless feet;
I think of you and wonder much
               when you and I shall meet⋯
Alas tonight I cannot pour my feelings forth in verse!

# 夜泊牛渚怀古

牛渚西江夜,青天无片云。
登舟望秋月,空忆谢将军。
余亦能高咏,斯人不可闻。
明朝挂帆去,枫叶落纷纷。

——[唐] 李白

【今译】

　　夜里将舟停泊在西江的牛渚山旁,蔚蓝的天空中没有一丝云彩。登上小船举头仰望天上的秋月,陡然想起了东晋的谢尚将军。我也能像袁宏一样吟咏高歌,可惜没有当年的谢将军来听。明天一早我将升起船帆离开了,这里只剩下枫叶飘落纷纷。

# 姑孰十咏·丹阳湖(节选)

[唐] 李白

龟游莲叶上,鸟宿芦花里。
少女棹轻舟,歌声逐流水。

## GENERAL HSIEH AN[①]

I anchor at the Newchew hill,
The autumn sky serene and still,
And watch the moon her crescent fill,
And vainly think on him by whom
this shore was made renowned.
Though mine is no ungraceful lay,
He cannot hear the words I say.
And I must sail at break of day
And all this while the maple leaves
are fluttering to the ground.

【注】 ①此处"HSIEH AN"系译者误译,应为"HSIEH SHANG"。

## A SNAP-SHOT

A tortoise I see on a lotus-flower resting:
A bird 'mid the reeds and the rushes is nesting;

【今译】

　　乌龟游到了莲叶上面,鸟儿栖息在芦花丛中。少女驾着小舟在轻轻地划水,歌声飘扬像在追逐着流水。

# 送 友 人

〔唐〕李白

　　青山横北郭,白水绕东城。
　　此地一为别,孤蓬万里征。
　　浮云游子意,落日故人情。
　　挥手自兹去,萧萧班马鸣。

【今译】

　　连绵的青山横亘在北城门外,清澈的河水环绕着东城。在这里我们就要分别了,你就像孤独的飞蓬即将漂泊在万里之外了。飘浮不定的白云正如你那游子的心意,西边的落日就像我不忍离别的心情。彼此挥手就此告别吧,你胯下的孤马也发出了依依不舍的嘶鸣。

A light skiff propelled by some boatman's fair daughter,
Whose song dies away o'er the fast-flowing water.


# A FAREWELL

Where blue hills cross the northern sky,
Beyond the moat which girds the town,
'Twas there we stopped to say Goodbye!
And one white sail alone dropped down.
Your heart was full of wandering thought;
For me, — my sun had set indeed;
To wave a last adieu we sought,
Voiced for us by each whinnying steed!

## 古朗月行

[唐] 李白

小时不识月，呼作白玉盘。
又疑瑶台镜，飞在白云端。
仙人垂两足，桂树作团团。
白兔捣药成，问言与谁餐。
蟾蜍蚀圆影，大明夜已残。
羿昔落九乌，天人清且安。
阴精此沦惑，去去不足观。
忧来其如何，凄怆摧心肝。

**【今译】**

　　小时不认识天上的月亮，把它叫作白玉盘。又怀疑它是瑶台神仙的镜子，飞到夜空中的云朵上面。月中的仙人是垂着双脚吗？月中的桂树为何如此的圆！白兔捣成了不老仙药，请问是给谁吃呢？蟾蜍把圆月咬得残缺不全，明亮的月儿因此变得晦暗。后羿曾经射落了九个太阳，天上人间才得以清明平安。此刻的月亮因沦没而迷惑不清，没有什么可欣赏的，不如远远走开吧。但又心怀忧虑不忍一走了之，眼前凄惨的景象使我暗自悲伤。

## BOYHOOD FANCIES

In days gone by the moon appeared
    to my still boyish eyes
Some bright jade plate or mirror from
    the palace of the skies.
I used to see the Old Man's legs
    and Cassias fair as gods can make them,
I saw the White Hare pounding drugs,
    and wondered who was there to take them.
Ah, how I watched the eclipsing Toad,
    and marked the ravages it made,
And longed for him who slew the suns
    and all the angels' fears allayed.
Then when the days of waning came,
    and scarce a silver streak remained,
I wept to lose my favourite thus,
    and cruel grief my eyelids stained.

## 玉 阶 怨

〔唐〕李白

玉阶生白露,夜久侵罗袜。
却下水晶帘,玲珑望秋月。

【今译】

　　玉石砌的台阶上生起了露水,罗袜因在深夜久立而被露水浸湿了。回到屋里放下水晶门帘,仍然隔着帘子凝望这一轮秋月。

## 山中问答

〔唐〕李白

问余何意栖碧山,笑而不答心自闲。
桃花流水窅然①去,别有天地非人间。

【今译】

　　有人问我为什么居住在碧山,我微笑不语,心中十分悠闲。溪水载着飘落的桃花向远方流去,这里别有一番天地,真不像身在人间。

【注】　①窅(yǎo)然:幽深遥远的样子。

## FROM THE PALACE

Cold dews of night the terrace crown,
And soak my stockings and my gown;
I'll step behind
The crystal blind,
And watch the autumn moon sink down.

## THE POET

You ask what my soul does away in the sky,
I inwardly smile but I cannot reply;
Like the peach-blossom carried away by the stream,
I soar to a world of which you cannot dream.

古今诗选

# 怨　情

[唐] 李白

美人卷珠帘，深坐颦蛾眉。
但见泪痕湿，不知心恨谁。

【今译】

　　美人卷起了珠帘，久坐不起还皱着蛾眉。只见她脸上泪痕斑斑，不知心里在怨恨谁。

# 宫中行乐词(其一)

[唐] 李白

小小生金屋，盈盈在紫微。
山花插宝髻，石竹绣罗衣。
每出深宫里，常随步辇归。
只愁歌舞散，化作彩云飞。

【今译】

　　从小生长在金屋里，拥有轻盈的舞姿，经常在皇帝面前表演。发髻上佩戴着美丽的山花，身上穿的是绣着山竹的罗

## TEARS

A fair girl draws the blind aside
And sadly sits with drooping head;
I see her burning tear-drops glide
But know not why those tears are shed.

## A FAVOURITE

Oh the joy of youth spent in a gold-fretted hall,
In the Crape-flower Pavilion, the fairest of all,
My tresses for headdress with gay garlands girt,
Carnations arranged o'er my jacket and skirt!
Then to wander away in the soft-scented air,
And return by the side of his Majesty's chair⋯
But the dance and the song will be o'er by and by,
And we shall dislimn like the rack in the sky.

衣。每每出入行走在深宫之中，常常伴随着皇帝的步辇而行。只怕有朝一日歌舞散尽，自己便像天上的彩云随风飘散，再也见不到皇帝了。

# 客 中 作

[唐] 李白

兰陵美酒郁金香，玉碗盛来琥珀光。
但使主人能醉客，不知何处是他乡。

【今译】

　　兰陵的美酒散发着浓郁的香气，盛在玉碗里现出琥珀的光泽。只要主人能让客人饮醉，客人就不会感到自己身在他乡。

# 秋浦歌(其十五)

[唐] 李白

白发三千丈，缘愁似个长。
不知明镜里，何处得秋霜。

## IN EXILE

I drink deep draughts of Lan-ling wine
        fragrant with borage made,
The liquid amber mantling up
        in cups of costly jade.
My host insists on making me
        as drunk as any sot,
Until I'm quite oblivious
        of the exile's wretched lot.

## IN A MIRROR

My whitening hair would make a long long rope,
Yet could not fathom all my depth of woe,

**【今译】**

　　白发长达三千丈，是因为愁才长得这样长。一尘不染的明镜里，不知是哪里飘来的秋霜落到了我的头上？

# 月下独酌（其一）

[唐] 李白

　　花间一壶酒，独酌无相亲。
　　举杯邀明月，对影成三人。
　　月既不解饮，影徒随我身。
　　暂伴月将影，行乐须及春。
　　我歌月徘徊，我舞影零乱。
　　醒时同交欢，醉后各分散。
　　永结无情游，相期邈云汉。

**【今译】**

　　在花丛中摆了一壶美酒，没有亲友的陪伴我只好自斟自饮。举起酒杯邀请明月一起共饮，明月、我和影子正好成了三个人。月亮当然不懂饮酒的快乐，身影也只是徒然伴随着我。只能把它们暂时作为酒伴吧，想及时行乐就必须趁着这明媚的春天。我引吭高歌，月亮随我来回移动，我翩翩起舞，在月光下身影纷乱。清醒时我们一起欢乐吧，酒醉后我们各

Though how it comes within a mirror's scope
To sprinkle autumn frosts, I do not know.

# LAST WORDS

An arbour of flowers and a kettle of wine:
Alas! in the bowers no companion is mine.
Then the moon sheds her rays on my goblet and me,
And my shadow betrays we're a party of three!
Though the moon cannot swallow her share of the grog,
And my shadow must follow wherever I jog, —
Yet their friendship I'll borrow and gaily carouse,
And laugh away sorrow while spring-time allows.
See the moon, — how she glances response to my song;
See my shadow, — it dances so lightly along!
While sober I feel, you are both my good friends;
When drunken I reel, our companionship ends.
But we'll soon have a greeting without a goodbye.
At our next merry meeting away in the sky.

自离散。不妨结成不会有伤心之情的游伴,相约在遥远的天上云端。

# 绝句二首(其二)

[唐] 杜甫

江碧鸟逾白,山青花欲燃。
今春看又过,何日是归年?

【今译】

　　碧绿的江水衬托得水鸟的羽毛越发雪白,盛开在郁郁葱葱的山岭上的鲜花红艳似火。眼看着今年的春天又要过去了,何年何月何日才是我归乡的日期啊?

# 落　日

[唐] 杜甫

落日在帘钩,溪边春事幽。
芳菲缘岸圃,樵爨①倚滩舟。

## IN ABSENCE

White gleam the gulls across the darkling tide,
On the green hills the red flowers seem to burn;
Alas! I see another spring has died...
When will it come — the day of my return?

## WINE

The setting sun shines low upon my door
Ere dusk enwraps the river fringed with spring;

古今诗选

喧雀争枝坠,飞虫满院游。
浊醪谁造汝,一酌散千忧。

【今译】

夕阳好像悬挂在窗帘的钩子上一样,窗外,农夫在小溪边忙着春耕。溪边河岸上的园圃里长满了花草,人们在溪滩的小船旁生火做饭。鸣叫的小鸟在枝头上追逐跳跃,飞虫在院子里来回翻飞不停。是谁酿造了这诱人的浊酒,喝了能解除千古之愁。

【注】 ①樵爨(cuàn):指烧火做饭的人。

# 月夜忆舍弟

[唐] 杜甫

戍鼓断人行,秋边一雁声。
露从今夜白,月是故乡明。
有弟皆分散,无家问死生。
寄书长不避,况乃未休兵。

【今译】

戍楼上的鼓声提醒人们不能再行走,深秋的边塞天空中

Sweet perfumes rise from gardens by the shore,
And smoke, where crews their boats to anchor bring.
Now twittering birds are roosting in the bower,
And flying insects fill the air around...
O wine, who gave to thee thy subtle power? —
A thousand cares in one small goblet drowned!

## TO HIS BROTHER

The evening drum has emptied every street,
One autumn goose screams on its frontier flight,
The crystal dew is glittering at my feet,
The moon sheds, as of old, her silvery light.
The brothers, — ah, where are they? Scattered each;
No home whence one might learn the other's harms.
Letters have oft miscarried: shall they reach

> 古今诗选

一只孤雁在鸣叫。从今夜开始就进入白露节气,月亮还是故乡的更为明亮。我的兄弟们都已经分散各地了,大家不在一起,彼此不知是生是死。寄往家里的书信经常不能送到,更何况现在战乱尚未结束。

# 江　村

### ［唐］杜甫

清江一曲抱村流,长夏江村事事幽。
自去自来堂上燕,相亲相近水中鸥。
老妻画纸为棋局,稚子敲针作钓钩。
多病所须唯药物,微躯此外更何求。

【今译】

　　清清的江水绕着村庄曲折流过,漫长的夏日,村里的一切都显得那么幽深。梁上的燕子飞来飞去、来去自由,水面上的鸥鸟很亲密地相伴相随。相伴多年的妻子正在用纸画着棋盘,儿子敲弯了针制作鱼钩。年老多病之躯所需的唯有药物,除此以外我还有什么奢求呢?

Now when the land rings with the clash of arms?

# HOME JOYS

My home is girdled by a limpid stream,
And there in summer days life's movements pause,
Save where some swallow flits from beam to beam,
And the wild sea-gull near and nearer draws.

The good wife rules a paper board for chess;
The children beat a fish-hook out of wire;
My ailments call for physic more or less,
What else should this poor frame of mine require?

# 琴　台

[唐] 杜甫

茂陵多病后，尚爱卓文君。
酒肆人间世，琴台日暮云。
野花留宝靥，蔓草见罗裙。
归凤求凰意，寥寥不复闻。

【今译】

　　司马相如已年老多病，仍然爱恋着卓文君。在市井开着酒舍，在琴台之上徘徊，欣赏碧空白云。那琴台旁的野花如同文君当年的笑容，碧绿的野草又如文君当年所穿的碧罗裙。司马相如追求卓文君的千古佳话，现在已经是很久不能再听到了。

# 题张氏隐居二首（其一）

[唐] 杜甫

春山无伴独相求，伐木丁丁山更幽。
涧道余寒历冰雪，石门斜日到林丘。
不贪夜识金银气，远害朝看麋鹿游。
乘兴杳然迷出处，对君疑是泛虚舟。

## SSU-MA HSIANG-JU

'Twas here, from sickness sore oppressed,
He found relief on  Wên-chün's breast;
'Twas here the vulgar tavern lay
On mountain cloud-capped night and day.
And still mid flowers and leaves I trace
Her fluttering robe, her tender face;
But ah! the phoenix calls in vain,
Such mate shall not be seen again.

## THE HERMIT

Alone I wandered o'er the hills
        to seek the hermit's den,
While sounds of chopping rang around
        the forest's leafy glen.

【今译】

  我在春日的山中独处无伴，因而特意拜访您，山中传来的丁丁的伐木声使山里更显得深幽。山涧通道上还留有寒气和积雪，走过石门古道，到达您隐居处已是夕阳西下时。您不贪图钱财夜间也不去观看金银之气，只想远离灾祸每日欣赏麋鹿嬉戏游走。我被您的情操感动得找不到来时的路，面对您就像乘上一只无人驾驶随意漂流的小舟。

# 曲江二首（其一）

[唐] 杜甫

一片花飞减却春，风飘万点正愁人。
且看欲尽花经眼，莫厌伤多酒入唇。
江上小堂巢翡翠，花边高冢卧麒麟。
细推物理须行乐，何用浮名绊此身。

【今译】

  仅一片花瓣的飘落便让人感到春色已减，狂风把千万朵

I passed on ice across the brook
        which had not ceased to freeze,
As the slanting rays of afternoon
        shot sparkling through the trees.
I found he did not joy to gloat
        o'er fetid wealth by night,
But far from taint, to watch the deer
        in the golden morning light...
My mind was clear at coming;
        but now I've lost my guide,
And rudderless my little bark
        is drifting with the tide!

## SOLO CHI SEGUE CIÒ CHE PIACE É SAGGIO[1]

A petal falls! — the spring begins to fail,
And my heart saddens with the growing gale.
Come then, ere autumn spoils bestrew the ground,
Do not forget to pass the wine-cup round.
Kingfishers build where man once laughed elate,
And now stone dragons guard his graveyard gate!
Who follows pleasure, he alone is wise;

花摇落在地，更令人心生忧伤。欣赏即将落尽的花瓣从眼前飘过，不要再厌烦更多的美酒入口。曲江上的楼堂里翡翠鸟正在筑巢，原来屹立的石麒麟现已倒卧在地。仔细探究世间万物的真理后发现，应该及时行乐，何必用虚幻的浮名来束缚自己呢？

# 曲江二首（其二）

[唐] 杜甫

朝回日日典春衣，每日江头尽醉归。
酒债寻常行处有，人生七十古来稀。
穿花蛱蝶深深见，点水蜻蜓款款飞。
传语风光共流转，暂时相赏莫相违。

【今译】

　　每日上朝归来，就去典当春天穿的衣服，然后去江边买酒喝，不醉不归。欠着的酒债都是寻常小事，人生在世能活到七十岁也是很少见的。蝴蝶飞舞在花丛深处，蜻蜓在水面上慢慢地飞，时不时点一下水。想传话给春光，让我们一起逗留，虽然是暂时相聚也不要违背约定。

Why waste our life in deeds of high emprise?

【注】 ①此为意大利语,意思是"只有那些随心随性的人才是明智的"。

# DUM RES ET AETAS①

From the court every eve to the pawnshop I pass,
To come back from the river the drunkest of men;
As often as not I'm in debt for my glass; —
Well, few of us live to be threescore and ten.
The butterfly flutters from flower to flower,
The dragon-fly sips and springs lightly away,
Each creature is merry its brief little hour,
So let us enjoy our short life while we may.

【注】 ①此为加泰罗尼亚语,意为"一无所有"之意。

古今诗选

# 陪诸贵公子丈八沟携妓纳凉,晚际遇雨二首(其一)

[唐] 杜甫

落日放船好,轻风生浪迟。
竹深留客处,荷净纳凉时。
公子调冰水,佳人雪藕丝。
片云头上黑,应是雨催诗。

【今译】

太阳落山了,正是行船的好时候,微风吹在水面上,泛起阵阵波纹。岸边茂密的竹林是留客的好地方,荷花盛开的地方正适合歇息纳凉。公子们畅饮用冰调制的冷饮,貌美的歌伎们除去嫩藕的白丝。天上突然飘来了一片黑云,应是在催促大家该及时创作助兴的诗歌了。

# 石 壕 吏

[唐] 杜甫

暮投石壕村,有吏夜捉人。老翁逾墙走,老妇出门看。吏呼一何怒!妇啼一何苦!
听妇前致词:三男邺城戍。一男附书至,二男新战死。存者且偷生,死者长已矣!室中更无人,惟有乳下孙。有孙

## A PICNIC

The sun is setting as we loose the boat,
And lightly o'er the breeze-swept waters float.
We seek a corner where the bamboo grows,
And fragrant lilies offer cool repose.
Here well-iced draughts of wine the men prepare,
With lotus shredded fine by fingers fair...
But now a black cloud gathering in the sky
Warns me to finish off my verse and fly.

## THE PRESSGANG

There, where at eve I sought a bed,
A pressgang came, recruits to hunt;
Over the wall the goodman sped,
And left his wife to bear the brunt.

古今诗选

母未去,出入无完裙。老妪力虽衰,请从吏夜归。急应河阳役,犹得备晨炊。夜久语声绝,如闻泣幽咽。天明登前途,独与老翁别。

【今译】

　　我傍晚投宿在石壕村,遇见官府差役夜里到村里来强行征兵。老翁吓得越墙逃跑了,老妇出门看情况。差役们大声威吓多么凶狠!老妇人放声大哭极其可怜!

　　我听到老妇上前说:"我的三个儿子都在邺城服役。一个儿子捎信回来,说另外两个儿子刚刚战死。能活着姑且活一天算一天吧,死去的人永远都不会复活。我家里没有其他人了,只有一个还在吃奶的小孙子。有孙子在,所以他母亲尚未改嫁,在家里进进出出连一件完整的衣服都没有。老妇我虽然年老力衰,但请连夜带我到军营吧。勉强应付一下河阳派来的急差,至少还能在军营为将士们准备早餐。老妇人说话的声音随着夜深逐渐听不见了,但隐约还能听到时断时续的哭泣声。我天亮出发离开石壕村时,只能同那个老翁道别了。

Ah me! the cruel serjeant's rage!
Ah me! how sadly she anon
Told all her story's mournful page, —
How three sons to the war had gone;

How one had sent a line to say
That two had been in battle slain:
He, from the fight had run away,
But they could ne'er come back again;

She swore 'twas all the family —
Except a grandson at the breast;
His mother too was there, but she
Was all in rags and tatters drest.

The crone with age was troubled sore,
But for herself she'd not think twice
To journey to the seat of war
And help to cook the soldiers' rice.

The night wore on and stopped her talk;
Then sobs upon my hearing fell...
At dawn when I set forth to walk,
Only the goodman cried Farewell!

古今诗选

## 绝句漫兴九首(其五)

[唐] 杜甫

肠断春江欲尽头,杖藜徐步立芳洲。
颠狂柳絮随风舞,轻薄桃花逐水流。

【今译】

　　春江景物美不胜收,站在江边感伤春天即将结束,拄着拐杖漫步江边,站在芳洲上望四周。漫天的柳絮随风飘舞,轻盈的桃花落在水中随波逐流。

## 题破山寺后禅院

[唐] 常建

清晨入古寺,初日照高林。
曲径通幽处,禅房花木深。
山光悦鸟性,潭影空人心。
万籁此都寂,但余钟磬音。

## SPRING JOYS[①]

When freshets cease in early spring
    and the river dwindles low,
I take my staff and wander
  by the banks where wild flowers grow.
I watch the willow-catkins
    wildly whirled on every side;
I watch the falling peach-bloom
    lightly floating down the tide.

【注】 ①此首诗译者原误认为是韦应物的诗,编者在此特修订并做注明。

## DHYANA

The clear dawn creeps into the convent old,
The rising sun tips its tall trees with gold, —
As, darkly, by a winding path I reach
Dhyana's hall, hidden midst fir and beech.

**【今译】**

  清晨我走进这个古老的寺院,初升的太阳照着高高的树林。蜿蜒的小路通向幽深的远处,禅房旁边的花草枝繁叶盛。山上的风景让鸟儿更加欢乐,深深的潭水让人气定神闲。此刻的我觉得万物静寂,只有敲钟击磬的余音回荡在心中。

# 宫 中 词

[唐] 朱庆馀

寂寂花时闭院门,美人相并立琼轩。
含情欲说宫中事,鹦鹉前头不敢言。

**【今译】**

  鲜花盛开在紧闭的宫门里,华美的走廊里美人们相依站立。她们满怀幽情想聊一些宫中的事儿,又怕学舌的鹦鹉偷听,而不敢开口。

Around these hills sweet birds their pleasure take,
Man's heart as free from shadows as this lake;
Here worldly sounds are hushed, as by a spell,
Save for the booming of the altar bell.

## IN THE HAREM

It was the time of flowers, the gate was closed;
Within an arbour's shade fair girls reposed.
But though their hearts were full, they nothing said,
Fearing the tell-tale parrot overhead.

## 别卢秦卿

[唐] 司空曙

知有前期在,难分此夜中。
无将故人酒,不及石尤风。

【今译】

尽管约定了下次见面的日期,可此夜之别仍然难舍难分。请不要拒绝我敬给你的酒,想要挽留你,却始终比不上那能阻止船只航行的顶头逆风。

## 春思二首(其一)

[唐] 贾至

草色青青柳色黄,桃花历乱李花香。
东风不为吹愁去,春日偏能惹恨长。

【今译】

春天里,碧草青青,柳树发芽;枝头上,桃花盛开,李花飘香。拂面的东风不能为我吹去忧愁,在这春天里,我的烦恼忧伤却不停地滋长。

## OH STAY

We shall meet, I believe you, again;
Yet to part! — such a beautiful night...
Shall friendship and wine ask in vain
What a head-wind would take as its right?

## SPRING SORROWS

The willow sprays are yellow fringed,
      the grass is gaily green;
Peach-blooms in wild confusion
      with the perfumed plum are seen;
The eastern breeze sweeps past me,
      yet my sorrows never go,
And the lengthening days of spring to me
      mean lengthening days of woe.

古今诗选

## 滁州西涧

[唐] 韦应物

独怜幽草涧边生,上有黄鹂深树鸣。
春潮带雨晚来急,野渡无人舟自横。

【今译】

　　我独喜欢欣赏在涧边生长的小草,还有在幽深树丛中鸣叫的黄鹂鸟。傍晚,春雨夹着潮水奔腾而下,野外渡口无人,只有一只小船横在江心。

## 秋夜寄邱员外

[唐] 韦应物

怀君属秋夜,散步咏凉天。
山空松子落,幽人应未眠。

【今译】

　　在这秋天的夜晚想起了你,一边散步一边感慨秋夜的凉意。寂静的山中能听到松子掉落的声音,隐居山中的你此刻应该也没有入睡。

## SUPERSEDED

Alas for the lonely plant that grows
            beside the river bed,
While the mango-bird screams loud and long
            from the tall tree overhead!
Full with the freshets of the spring,
            the torrent rushes on;
The ferry-boat swings idly, for
            the ferryman is gone.

## REMEMBRANCES

In autumn, when the nights are chill,
I stroll, and croon, and think of thee.
When dropping pine-cones strew the hill,
Say, hast thou waking dreams of me?

## 寄李儋元锡

[唐] 韦应物

去年花里逢君别,今日花开又一年。
世事茫茫难自料,春愁黯黯独成眠。
身多疾病思田里,邑有流亡愧俸钱。
闻道欲来相问讯,西楼望月几回圆?

【今译】

　　去年在花开季节和你分别,现在又到花开季节,我们分开已一年了。茫茫人世间很多事都不能预料,在这春愁的季节里,心中郁郁,孤枕难眠。身体多病的我很想归隐田园,看到邑内百姓生活困苦,使我感到愧对国家的俸禄。听说你最近要来和我相见,我登上西楼独自望月,几度看到明月圆。

## A PROMISE

Sweet flowers were blooming all around
        when your last farewell you said,
And now the opening buds proclaim
        another year has fled.
'Tis difficult to prophesy
        beyond the present day,
And the remedy for trouble
        is to sleep it all away.
I suffer much in body,
        and I long for the old spot,
But cannot bring myself in pensioned
        idleness to rot.
You say that you will visit me,
        that you are coming soon:
'Twixt now and then how often
        shall I see the full-orbed moon?

## 登总持阁

[唐] 岑参

高阁逼诸天,登临近日边。
晴开万井树,愁看五陵烟。
槛外低秦岭,窗中小渭川。
早知清净理,常愿奉金仙。

【今译】

　　总持阁高耸入云直插天空,登上楼阁仿佛靠近了日边。晴天的时候,街道市井尽收眼底,远处五陵之上涌起的烟雾使人心生愁思。凭靠栏杆,看那秦岭显得又低又矮;站在窗边,看那渭水变得细小绵长。我早已知晓清净之理,所以愿时刻侍奉在佛的身边。

## 凉州词二首(其一)

[唐] 王翰

葡萄美酒夜光杯,欲饮琵琶马上催。
醉卧沙场君莫笑,古来征战几人回。

## BUDDHISM

A shrine, whose eaves in far-off cloudland hide:
I mount, and with the sun stand side by side.
The air is clear; I see wide forests spread
And mist-crowned heights where Kings of old lie dead.
Scarce o'er my threshold peeps the Southern Hill;
The Wei shrinks through my window to a rill...
O thou Pure Faith, had I but known thy scope,
The Golden God had long since been my hope!

## A REASON FAIR

'Tis night: the grape-juice mantles high
        in cups of gold galore;
We set to drink, — but now the bugle
        sounds to horse once more.

古今诗选

【今译】

　　醇美的葡萄酒盛在夜光杯里,将士们正要畅饮时,马上琵琶声声响起,催人出征。即使醉倒在战场上也不要笑话,从古到今征战的将士又有几人能全身而归。

## 秋　日

[唐] 耿湋

反照入闾巷,忧来与谁语?
古道无人行,秋风动禾黍。

【今译】

　　夕阳的余晖照进幽深的巷子,我满腹的忧伤能和谁说呢?荒凉的古道上很少见到行人,唯见秋风吹动路旁的庄稼。

## 经漂母墓

[唐] 刘长卿

昔贤怀一饭,兹事已千秋。

Oh marvel not if drunken
        we lie strewed about the plain;
How few of all who seek the fight
        shall e'er come back again!

## LONELY

The evening sun slants o'er the village street;
My griefs alas! in solitude are borne;
Along the road no wayfarers I meet, —
Naught but the autumn breeze across the corn.

## THE WASHERWOMAN'S GRAVE

The hero ne'er forgot the meal she gave, —

古墓樵人识，前朝楚水流。
渚蘋行客荐，山木杜鹃愁。
春草茫茫绿，王孙旧此游。

【今译】

　　从前的贤士为感念一顿饭而报恩，这件事情已经过去千年。古时留下的漂母的坟墓，打柴人还能认出，楚地的河流从前朝一直流到如今。小洲上的蘋草成为行人的席垫，林中的杜鹃鸟发出悲愁的鸣声。春草一片碧绿长得十分繁盛，清高的隐士来到这里旧地重游。

# 伊 州 歌

〔唐〕盖嘉运

打起黄莺儿，莫教枝上啼。
啼时惊妾梦，不得到辽西。

【今译】

　　敲打树枝赶走树上的黄莺吧，别让它在枝头上啼鸣；它啼叫的声音惊醒了我的好梦，使我不能在梦里到辽西和丈夫相聚。

My tale is of a thousand years ago, —
And every woodsman knows the time-worn grave,
Though naught remains of dynasties save
              the river's ceaseless flow.
With votive flower the traveller is seen,
The while the grief-bird trills his mournful lays;
Around, the grass of spring grows wildly green
Where footprints of the "nobleman"
              were left in bygone days.

## AT DAWN

Drive the young orioles away,
Nor let them on the branches play;
Their chirping breaks my slumber through
And keeps me from my dreams of you.

古今诗选

## 同王徵君湘中有怀句

[唐] 张谓

八月洞庭秋,潇湘水北流。
还家万里梦,为客五更愁。
不用开书帙,偏宜上酒楼。
故人京洛满,何日复同游?

【今译】

　　八月的洞庭湖进入了秋天,湘江和潇水滔滔向北流去。回家是远在万里之外的我的一个梦想,身处他乡为客,五更时分又泛起乡愁。不用打开书卷阅读典籍,最好是去酒楼借酒消愁。我的故人遍布长安和洛阳,哪一天才能和他们一起开心畅游呢?

## 闺　　怨

[唐] 王昌龄

闺中少妇不知愁,春日凝妆上翠楼。
忽见陌头杨柳色,悔教夫婿觅封侯。

## NOSTALGIA

'Tis autumn, and I watch the streams
Which towards my dear home flow;
I span the distance in my dreams,
And wake to deeper woe.
I cannot read to ease my care.
But solace seek in wine,
And think of friends all gathered there —
When will that lot be mine?

## AT THE WARS

See the young wife whose bosom ne'er
    has ached with cruel pain! —
In gay array she mounts the tower

古今诗选

【今译】

　　闺中的少妇不知道忧和愁,在明媚的春天里,她盛装打扮登上翠楼。忽然看见路边的杨柳冒出了新绿,心里十分懊悔让丈夫远离家乡去建功封侯。

# 芙蓉楼送辛渐

## [唐] 王昌龄

寒雨连江夜入吴,平明送客楚山孤。
洛阳亲友如相问,一片冰心在玉壶。

【今译】

　　在冷雨洒向江面的半夜,我来到了吴地,天亮送别客人后,楚山显得格外孤独。洛阳的亲朋好友如果问起我,就说我的心像玉壶里的冰块一样纯洁无瑕。

when spring comes round again.
Sudden she sees the willow-trees
            their newest green put on,
And sighs for her husband far away
            in search of glory gone.


# A MESSAGE

Onwards tonight my storm-beat course I steer,
At dawn these mountains will for ever fade;
Should those I leave behind enquire my cheer,
Tell them, "an icy heart in vase of jade."

## 苏氏别业

[唐] 祖咏

别业居幽处，到来生隐心。
南山当户牖，沣水映园林。
屋覆经冬雪，庭昏未夕阴。
寥寥人境外，闲坐听春禽。

**【今译】**

　　这个别墅地处幽静的地方，来到这里自然就会心生隐居之意。透过门窗能看到远处的南山，流经的沣水映照着园林的景色。竹子上还覆盖着冬天的残雪，还没到黄昏院子里已满是暮色。这种幽静的环境仿佛远离了人间，可以静静地坐着闲听春鸟的啼鸣。

## 题都城南庄

[唐] 崔护

去年今日此门中，人面桃花相映红。
人面不知何处去，桃花依旧笑春风。

## A GROTTO

Deep in a darksome grove their Grotto lies,
And deep the thoughts that now within me rise.
Fronting the door the South Hill looming near,
The forest mirrored in the river clear,
The bamboo bends beneath last winter's snow,
The court-yard darkens ere the day sinks low.
I seem to pass beyond this world of clay,
And sit and listen to the spring-bird's lay.

## A RETROSPECT

Oh this day last year what a party were we
Pink cheeks and pink peach-blossoms smiled upon me;
But alas the pink cheeks are now far far away,

古今诗选

【今译】

　　去年的今天我来到这户人家,姑娘的美貌和鲜艳的桃花交相互映。如今这个姑娘不知去往何处,只有树上的桃花在春风中怒放盛开。

# 玉 台 体

[唐] 权德舆

昨夜裙带解,今朝蟢子飞。
铅华不可弃,莫是藁砧归。

【今译】

　　昨夜我的裙带莫名松弛解开了,今早起床又见蟢子双双飞舞。还是尽快梳妆打扮一番吧,莫不是我的丈夫就要回家了吧。

Though the peach-blossoms smile as they
                              smiled on that day.

# HOPE

Last eve thou wert a bride,
This morn thy dream is o'er...
Cast not thy rouge aside,
He may be thine once more.

# 病　鸱

[唐] 韩愈

屋东恶水沟，有鸱堕鸣悲。青泥掩两翅，拍拍不得离。
君童叫相召，瓦砾争先之。计校生平事，杀却理亦宜。
夺攘不愧耻，饱满盘天嬉。晴日占光景，高风恣追随。
遂凌鸾凤群，肯顾鸿鹄卑。今者命运穷，遭逢巧丸儿。
中汝要害处，汝能不得施。于吾乃何有，不忍乘其危。
丐汝将死命，浴以清水池。朝餐辍鱼肉，暝宿防狐狸。
自知无以致，蒙德久犹疑。饱入深竹丛，饥来傍阶基。
亮无责报心，固以听所为。昨日有气力，飞跳弄藩篱。
今晨忽径去，曾不报我知。侥幸非汝福，天衢汝休窥。
京城事弹射，竖子不易欺。勿讳泥坑辱，泥坑乃良规。

**【今译】**

　　我家东边有一条臭水沟，一只鸱鸟掉进去了，正悲哀地鸣叫着。水沟里的污泥沾满了它的两只翅膀，它使劲拍打翅膀却飞不起来。儿童相互呼唤聚到这里，争先恐后地用瓦砾砸向鸱鸟。想想鸱鸟一生的所作所为，纵然被瓦砾砸死也是正当合理。

　　它抢夺食物从来不觉得自己羞愧可耻，只要吃饱了就会满天飞舞，不停戏耍。在风和日丽的晴天独占美景，起大风时它又随风恣意翱翔。还时常欺负鸾鸟和凤凰，也不肯去对比大雁和天鹅而感到自卑。

# THE WOUNDED FALCON

Within a ditch beyond my wall
I saw a falcon headlong fall.
Bedaubed with mud and racked with pain,
It beat its wings to rise, in vain;
While little boys threw tiles and stones,
Eager to break the wretch's bones.
O bird, methinks thy life of late
Hath amply justified this fate!
Thy sole delight to kill and steal,
And then exultingly to wheel,
Now sailing in the clear blue sky.
Now on the wild gale sweeping by,
Scorning thy kind of less degree
As all unfit to mate with thee.
But mark how fortune's wheel goes round;
A pellet lays thee on the ground,
Sore stricken at some vital part, —
And where is then thy pride of heart?
What's this to me? — I could not bear
To see the fallen one lying there.
I begged its life, and from the brook

## 古今诗选

时至今日它到了穷途末路，又遭遇善射弹丸的人。弹丸打中了它的要害之处，受伤后一身本领也无从施展发挥。对于我来说也没有其他想法，只是不忍心乘其危难而加害于它。所以向儿童请求饶它一命，在清水池里把它洗得干干净净。早餐不用鱼和肉喂它，夜晚睡觉还防止狐狸来伤害它。它也自知没有什么能报答我，蒙受我的恩惠时间虽长仍心存疑虑。吃饱了就钻进竹林深处，饿了就来到房前台阶旁边。我救它并没有要求回报的想法，所以就由它来去自由任其所为。昨天它似乎恢复了气力，便在藩篱前飞飞跳跳。今天早上它忽然径自飞走，也没有和我打个招呼。

侥幸遇救并不一定是鸥鸟的福分，海阔天空但也不要任意妄为。京城里善于弹射的人很多，即使年少的人也不要瞧不起。请不要避讳自己在泥坑中屈辱的经历，那段经历正是对你的良言忠告。

Water to wash its wounds I took.
Fed it with bits of fish by day,
At night from foxes kept away.
My care I knew would naught avail
For gratitude, that empty tale.
And so this bird would crouch and hide
Till want its stimulus applied;
And I, with no reward to hope,
Allowed its callousness full scope.
Last eve the bird showed signs of rage,
With health renewed, and beat its cage.
Today it forced a passage through,
And took its leave, without adieu.
Good luck hath saved thee, not desert;
Beware, O bird, of further hurt;
Beware the archer's deadly tools! —
'Tis hard to escape the shafts of fools —
Nor e'er forget the chastening ditch
That found thee poor, and left thee rich.

古今诗选

# 读皇甫湜公安园池诗书其后二首(其二)

[唐] 韩愈

我有一池水,蒲苇生其间。
虫鱼沸相嚼,日夜不得闲。
我初往观之,其后益不观。
观之乱我意,不如不观完。
用将济诸人,舍得业孔颜。
百年讵几时,君子不可闲。

【今译】

  我有一个池塘,里面长了很多蒲苇。鱼儿和虫子在池中相互争斗,白天和黑夜都不停歇。我到池塘边去看看,看一眼后就随它们去了。看鱼虫争斗实在没什么意思,没必要把争斗的过程都看完。不如节省时间来帮助别人,用来习修圣人之道。人生百年岂可浪费时间,君子没有闲散的理由。

# 感春四首(其四)

[唐] 韩愈

我恨不如江头人,长网横江遮紫鳞。
独宿荒陂射凫雁,卖纳租赋官不嗔。

## HOURS OF IDLENESS

A little lake of mine I know,
Where waving weeds and rushes grow,
And in its depths by day and night
The water-monsters swarm and fight.
Ah, how I loved to idle there! ...
But now I can no longer bear
To pass my days in that sweet spot,
And lost in meditation rot.
A sense of duty gives me pause,
Obedient to my Master's laws;
Our span of life is all too short
To waste its hours in empty sport.

## DISCONTENT

To stand upon the river-bank
        and snare the purple fish,

### 古今诗选

归来欢笑对妻子,衣食自给宁羞贫。
今者无端读书史,智慧只足劳精神。
画蛇著足无处用,两鬓霜白趋埃尘。
乾愁漫解坐自累,与众异趣谁相亲。
数杯浇肠虽暂醉,皎皎万虑醒还新。
百年未满不得死,且可勤买抛青春。

**【今译】**

  我恨自己活得不如江边的打渔人,他们用大网横截江水来捕鱼。他们独自宿在荒凉的水边猎取野鸭,卖了后交纳租赋,这样就不会惹得官家生气。回家后和妻儿欢聚一堂,吃穿自给自足,不会因生活的贫困而羞愧。如今我疑惑自己当初为什么读那么多书,获得的知识只能使自己徒劳伤神。像画蛇添足一样没什么实际用途,两鬓都白了依然在人世间奔波操劳。不仅解不开莫名的忧愁,反而更受其拖累。与众人志趣不同实在是找不到可以倾诉的知音。几杯酒下肚后虽然能得到暂时的麻醉,可酒醒后难解的忧愁依然清清楚楚摆在面前。人生大限未到,暂时还死不了,那就继续多买些酒喝,不辜负这美好的春天。

My net well cast across the stream,
>   was all that I could wish.
Or lie concealed and shoot the geese
>   that scream and pass apace,
And pay my rent and taxes with
>   the profits of the chase.
Then home to peace and happiness,
>   with wife and children gay,
Though clothes be coarse and fare be hard,
>   and earned from day to day.
But now I read and read, scarce knowing
>   what 'tis all about,
And eager to improve my mind
>   I wear my body out.
I draw a snake and give it legs,
>   to find I've wasted skill,
And my hair grows daily whiter
>   as I hurry towards the hill.
I sit amid the sorrows
>   I have brought on my own head,
And find myself estranged from all,
>   among the living dead.
I seek to drown my consciousness
>   in wine, alas! in vain:
Oblivion passes quickly

# 杂诗四首（其一）

[唐] 韩愈

朝蝇不须驱，暮蚊不可拍。
蝇蚊满八区，可尽与相格。
得时能几时，与汝恣啖咋。
凉风九月到，扫不见踪迹。

【今译】

　　早上的苍蝇不用驱赶，晚上的蚊子不用拍打。四面八方都是蚊蝇，和它们斗争起来没有尽头。且让它们得意时就得意，让它们随便咬叮吧，待到九月冷风起，它们不需要理会就会消失得无影无踪。

and my griefs' begin again.
Old age comes on and yet withholds
　　　the summons to depart⋯
So I'll take another bumper
　　　just to ease my aching heart.


# HUMANITY

Oh spare the busy morning fly!
Spare the mosquitos of the night!
And if their wicked trade they ply
Let a partition stop their flight.

Their span is brief from birth to death;
Like you they bite their little day;
And then, with autumn's earliest breath,
Like you too they are swept away.

## 杂曲歌辞·少年乐

[唐] 李贺

芳草落花如锦地,二十长游醉乡里。
红缨不重白马骄,垂柳金丝香拂水。
吴娥未笑花不开,绿鬟耸堕兰云起。
陆郎倚醉牵罗袂,夺得宝钗金翡翠。

**【今译】**

　　掉落的花朵和青草如同在地上铺了一层织锦,二十岁的少年酒醉后在长时间游玩。骑着矫健飞驰的白马,手里的缰绳变得十分轻松;岸边柳树垂下金黄的柳丝轻拂着河水。吴地的美女不笑时,似乎花儿也不绽放了。美女们乌黑光亮的鬟发像云朵一样随风飘起。少年像陆郎一样仗着酒意大胆牵扯美女的衣袖,顺手摘到美女头上戴的宝钗和手上戴的翡翠手镯。

## 秋风引

[唐] 刘禹锡

何处秋风至?萧萧送雁群。
朝来入庭树,孤客最先闻。

## NEAERA'S TANGLES

With flowers on the ground like embroidery spread,
At twenty, the soft glow of wine in my head,
My white courser's bit-tassels motionless gleam
While the gold-threaded willow scent sweeps
                        o'er the stream.
Yet until she has smiled all these flowers yield no ray,
When her tresses fall down, the whole landscape is gay;
My hand on her sleeve as I gaze in her eyes,
A kingfisher hairpin will soon be my prize.

## SUMMER DYING

Whence comes the autumn's whistling blast,
With flocks of wild geese hurrying past?⋯

【今译】

　　不知哪里来的秋风吹到这里,吹动着树梢送走了一群群大雁。早晨的秋风撩动院里的大树,孤独的异乡客人最先听到了声音。

# 和乐天春词

[唐] 刘禹锡

新妆宜面下朱楼,深锁春光一院愁。
行到中庭数花朵,蜻蜓飞上玉搔头。

【今译】

　　梳妆打扮一番走下绣楼,眼前春光满院却又显得忧愁。走到院中数着那开得正艳的花儿,一只蜻蜓却飞到了头戴的玉簪上面。

Alas, when wintry breezes burst,
The lonely traveller hears them first!

## THE ODALISQUE

A gaily dressed damsel steps forth from her bower,
Bewailing the fate that forbids her to roam;
In the courtyard she counts up the buds on each flower,
While a dragon-fly flutters and sits on her comb.

## 后 宫 词

[唐] 白居易

泪湿罗巾梦不成,夜深前殿按歌声。
红颜未老恩先断,斜倚薰笼坐到明。

【今译】

　　泪水打湿罗巾无法入睡,连个好梦也做不成,深夜时分,前殿仍然传来有韵律的歌声。年轻的妃子尚未衰老就失去了皇帝的恩宠,独自一人倚着熏笼孤独地坐到天明。


## 行 宫

[唐] 元稹

寥落古行宫,宫花寂寞红。
白头宫女在,闲坐说玄宗。

【今译】

　　在寂寞冷落的古旧行宫里,宫中的花寂寞地开放着。有几个头发已经花白的老宫女,坐着闲聊当年唐玄宗的事情。

## DESERTED

Soaked is her kerchief through with tears,
        yet slumber will not come;
In the deep dead of night she hears
        the song and beat of drum.

Alas, although his love has gone,
        her beauty lingers yet;
Sadly she sits till early dawn,
        but never can forget.

## AT AN OLD PALACE

Deserted now the Imperial bowers
Save by some few poor lonely flowers...
        One white-haired dame,
        An Emperor's flame,
Sits down and tells of bygone hours.

## 宫　怨

[唐] 李益

露湿晴花春殿香，月明歌吹在昭阳。
似将海水添宫漏，共滴长门一夜长。

【今译】

　　露水打湿了春晴正开的花朵，宫殿里满是幽香；明亮的月光下，昭阳殿歌舞不休。宫漏里的水像是大海一样怎么也滴不完，在长门宫前滴了一夜，显得时间是那么漫长。

## 节妇吟·寄东平李司空师道

[唐] 张籍

君知妾有夫，赠妾双明珠。
感君缠绵意，系在红罗襦。
妾家高楼连苑起，良人执戟明光里。
知君用心如日月，事夫誓拟同生死。
还君明珠双泪垂，何不相逢未嫁时。

## A CAST-OFF FAVOURITE

The dewdrops gleam on bright spring flowers
        whose scent is borne along;
        Beneath the moon the palace rings
        with sounds of lute and song.
It seems that the clepsydra
        has been filled up with the sea,
To make the long long night appear
        an endless night to me!

## THE CHASTE WIFE'S REPLY

Knowing, fair sir, my matrimonial thrall,
Two pearls thou sentest me, costly withal.
And I, seeing that Love thy heart possessed,
I wrapped them coldly in my silken vest.
For mine is a household of high degree.
My husband captain in the King's army;
And one with wit like thine should say,

古今诗选

**【今译】**

　　你知道我已经有了丈夫，却还要送给我一对明珠。谢谢你对我的绵绵情意，我把明珠系在红罗短裙上。我家的高楼紧挨着皇家园林，我丈夫手执长戟守卫着皇宫。我很清楚你对我是光明磊落，但我早已发誓和丈夫生死与共。把明珠退还给你的时候我不禁流下眼泪，只遗憾我没有在出嫁前遇见你啊。

# 城东早春

[唐] 杨巨源

诗家清景在新春，绿柳才黄半未匀。
若待上林花似锦，出门俱是看花人。

**【今译】**

　　向来为诗人最爱的秀丽景色在早春时节，碧绿的柳枝上嫩芽才开始变黄。若是到了长安城鲜花都盛开的时节，出门遇见全是赏花的人。

"The troth of wives is for ever and ay."
With thy two pearls I send thee back two tears:
Tears — that we did not meet in earlier years!

# TASTE

The landscape which the poet loves
        is that of early May,
When budding greenness half concealed
        enwraps each willow spray.
That beautiful embroidery
        the days of summer yield,
Appeals to every bumpkin
        who may take his walks afield.

## 怅　诗

［唐］杜牧

自是寻春去校迟，不须惆怅怨芳时。
狂风落尽深红色，绿叶成阴子满枝。

【今译】

　　遗憾自己去寻访春色太晚，不必惆怅抱怨花儿提前开放。虽然狂风吹落了红色的鲜花，但是绿叶繁茂，枝上果实累累。

## 金谷园

［唐］杜牧

繁华事散逐香尘，流水无情草自春。
日暮东风怨啼鸟，落花犹似坠楼人。

【今译】

　　繁华的往事随着芳香的烟尘已经散去，流水无情地流淌，小草依旧迎春自绿。日暮时的东风里传来鸟儿阵阵哀鸣，飘落的花朵好似那从楼上坠落的美人。

## A LOST LOVE

Too late, alas! I came to find
        the lovely spring had fled.
Yet must I not regret the days
        of youth that now are dead;
For though the rosy buds of spring
        the cruel winds have laid,
Behold the clustering fruit that hangs
        beneath the leafy shade!

## THE OLD PLACE

A wilderness alone remains,
        all garden glories gone;
The river runs unheeded by,
        weeds grow unheeded on.
Dusk comes, the east wind blows, and birds
        pipe forth a mournful sound;
Petals, like nymphs from balconies,
        come tumbling to the ground.

## 赠别二首（其二）

[唐] 杜牧

多情却似总无情，唯觉樽前笑不成。
蜡烛有心还惜别，替人垂泪到天明。

【今译】

多情的人却像无情的人一样冰冷，只觉得端起酒杯却无法把盏言欢。燃烧的蜡烛仿佛有依依惜别的心意，替离别的人一直流泪到天明。

## 七 夕

[唐] 杜牧

银烛秋光冷画屏，轻罗小扇扑流萤。
天阶夜色凉如水，卧看牵牛织女星。

【今译】

银烛的烛光照着冷清的画屏，手拿小罗扇轻轻扑打飞舞的萤火虫。深夜里的石阶清凉如冷水，躺在卧榻上静静仰视牵牛织女星。

## THE LAST NIGHT

Old love would seem as though not love today;
Spell-bound by thee, my laughter dies away.
The very wax sheds sympathetic tears
And gutters sadly down till dawn appears.

## LOVERS PARTED

Across the screen the autumn moon
        stares coldly from the sky;
With silken fan I sit and flick
        the fireflies sailing by.
The night grows colder every hour, —
        it chills me to the heart
To watch the Spinning Maiden
        from the Herdboy far apart.

古今诗选

## 登乐游原

[唐] 李商隐

向晚意不适,驱车登古原。
夕阳无限好,只是近黄昏。

【今译】

　　傍晚时分感觉心情不太舒畅,独自驾车登上了乐游原。眼前的夕阳晚景显得无限美好,可惜已临近黄昏。

## 夜雨寄北

[唐] 李商隐

君问归期未有期,巴山夜雨涨秋池。
何当共剪西窗烛,却话巴山夜雨时。

【今译】

　　你问我何时回家,我却定不下具体的日期,巴山夜里的雨水已经涨满了秋天的池塘。什么时候我们能一起坐在家里的西窗下剪着烛花,相互倾诉那巴山深夜下雨时的思念之情。

## THE NIGHT COMES

'Tis evening, and in restless vein
At the old mount I slacken rein:
    The glorious day
    Fades fast away
And naught but twilight glooms remain!


## SOUVENIRS

You ask when I'm coming: alas, not just yet...
How the rain filled the pools on that night
                      when we met!
Ah, when shall we ever snufF candles again,
And recall the glad hours of that evening of rain?

## 社 日

[唐] 张演

鹅湖山下稻粱肥,豚栅鸡栖对掩扉。
桑柘影斜春社散,家家扶得醉人归。

【今译】

　　鹅湖山下的稻粱肥硕,丰收在望,半开半掩的门里,每家都猪肥鸡壮。夕阳把桑树和柘树的影子拉出长长的影子,春社才结束,每家都搀扶着喝醉的人尽兴还家。

## 登 山

[唐] 李涉

终日昏昏醉梦间,忽闻春尽强登山。
因过竹院逢僧话,偷得浮生半日闲。

【今译】

　　整天昏昏沉沉恍若梦中,突然发现春天将尽,便强打精神去登山。路上经过一个种满竹子的院子,和僧人聊了起来,暂时忘掉烦恼,难得在这纷扰的世事中暂且得到半天的清闲。

## A SPRING FEAST

The paddy crops are waxing rich
        upon the Goose-Lake hill;
The fowls have just now gone to roost,
        the grunting pigs are still;
The mulberry casts a lengthening shade, —
        the festival is o'er,
And tipsy revellers are helped
        each to his cottage door.

## ESCAPE

Confusion overwhelming me,
        as in a drunken dream,
I note that spring has fled
        and wander off to hill and stream;
With a friendly Buddhist priest I seek
        a respite from the strife
And manifold anomalies
        which go to make up life.

古今诗选

## 井栏砂宿遇夜客

[唐] 李涉

暮雨潇潇江上村,绿林豪客夜知闻。
他时不用逃姓名,世上如今半是君。

【今译】

　　江边小村傍晚的时候风雨潇潇,深夜遇到的绿林好汉居然知道我的名字。将来你们这些绿林好汉不用隐姓埋名,逃避官府捉拿,现在社会上多半是像你们这样的人。

## 春　　晴

[唐] 王驾

雨前初见花间蕊,雨后全无叶底花。
蜂蝶纷纷过墙去,却疑春色在邻家。

【今译】

　　春雨之前还看到花间露出的新蕊,春雨后就连叶子底下也看不到一朵花。蜜蜂和蝴蝶接连不断飞过院墙,简直让我怀疑醉人的春色尽在邻居家中。

## ON HIGHWAYMEN

The rainy mist sweeps gently
      o'er the village by the stream,
When from the leafy forest glades
      the brigand daggers gleam...
And yet there is no need to fear
      or step from out their way,
For more than half the world consists
      of bigger rogues than they!

## A STORM

No rain, and lovely flowers bloom around;
Rain falls, and battered petals strew the ground.
The bees and butterflies flit, one and all,
To seek the spring beyond my neighbour's wall.

## 即 景

[宋] 朱淑真

竹摇清影罩幽窗,两两时禽噪夕阳。
谢却海棠飞尽絮,困人天气日初长。

【今译】

  微风摇动,竹影映在幽静的窗子上,成双成对的鸟儿在夕阳下飞舞鸣叫。海棠花开败了,柳絮也不见了踪影,在让人困倦的天气里,白天变得越来越长了。

## 落 花

[宋] 朱淑真

连理枝头花正开,妒花风雨便相催。
愿教青帝常为主,莫遣纷纷点翠苔。

【今译】

  连理枝上的花儿正在绽放,嫉妒鲜花的风雨催促它的凋谢。希望掌管春天的青帝能长久做主,别让美丽的花朵掉落到地面的青苔上。

## SUMMER BEGINS

What time the bamboo casts a deeper shade,
When birds fill up the afternoon with song,
When catkins vanish, and when pear-blooms fade, —
Then man is weary and the day is long.

## LOVE'S SPRINGTIME

Twin blossoms blooming on a single flower!...
Then comes the jealous storm with shattering sound.
Oh could we always feel the Spring-God's power,
No petals scattered on the moss-grown ground!

古今诗选

## 江楼感旧

〔唐〕赵嘏

独上江楼思渺然,月光如水水如天。
同来望月人何处?风景依稀似去年。

【今译】

　　我独自登上江边的小楼思绪怅然,月光像流水一样,江水澄莹如天。往日和我同来赏月的人现在在哪里呀?眼前的风景却一如去年。

## 除夜宿石头驿

〔唐〕戴叔伦

旅馆谁相问,寒灯独可亲。
一年将尽夜,万里未归人。
寥落悲前事,支离笑此身。
愁颜与衰鬓,明日又逢春。

【今译】

　　在这寂寞的旅店中有谁来看望,只有一盏孤灯和我做伴。

## WHERE ARE THEY?

Alone I mount to the kiosque which stands
      on the river-bank, and sigh,
While the moonbeams dance on the tops of the waves
      where the waters touch the sky;
For the lovely scene is to last year's scene
      as like as like can be.
All but the friends, the much-loved friends,
      who gazed at the moon with me.

## NEW YEAR'S EVE AT AN INN

Here in this inn no friend is nigh;
We sit alone, my lamp and I,
A thousand miles from love and smiles,
To see another year pass by.

Ah me, that ever I was born!
Is life worth living, thus forlorn?

今夜是一年中的最后一个夜晚,我还是那寄居万里之外回不了家的人。孤独寂寥的我对往事充满伤悲,与亲人分开让我苦笑中带着心酸。忧愁使我容颜变老、白了头发,明天还要迎接新春。

## 婕妤春怨

[唐] 皇甫冉

花枝出建章,凤管发昭阳。
借问承恩者,双蛾几许长。

【今译】

宫女们打扮得花枝招展,走出建章宫,到昭阳宫里表演歌舞。请问正受宠爱的美女们,你们的美貌能超过我多少。

## 秋日湖上

[唐] 薛莹

落日五湖游,烟波处处愁。
沈浮千古事,谁与问东流。

Youth, beauty, pass; and yet alas
It will be spring tomorrow morn.

## SPRETAE INJURIA FORMAE

See! fair girls are flocking, through
                       corridors bright,
With music and mirth borne along on
                       the breeze...
Come, tell me if she who is favoured
                       tonight
Has eyebrows much longer than these?

## MUSING

At eve, along the river bank,
The mist-crowned wavelets lure me on

**【今译】**

  落日时分在太湖泛舟游览，水上烟波浩渺，使人心生忧愁，千百年来如烟的历史浮浮沉沉，没有谁去问询那永不停息的向东而去的水流。

# 闻邻家理筝

### ［唐］徐安贞

  北斗横天夜欲阑，愁人倚月思无端。
  忽闻画阁秦筝逸，知是邻家赵女弹。
  曲成虚忆青蛾敛，调急遥怜玉指寒。
  银锁重关听未辟，不如眠去梦中看。

**【今译】**

  北斗七星横斜于天上，夜色更加深沉，满怀愁苦的人在月色下思绪万千。突然听到楼上传来阵阵弹筝声，应该是邻家的美女在弹奏吧。我猜美女应是双眉紧皱，玉指翻飞拨弄琴弦。只是阁楼的大门紧闭，无法进去聆听，不如尽快入睡，到梦里去看看她吧。

To think how all antiquity
Has floated down the stream and gone!

# MY NEIGHBOUR

When the Bear athwart was lying
And the night was just on dying,
And the moon was all but gone,
How my thoughts did ramble on!

Then a sound of music breaks
From a lute that some one wakes,
And I know that it is she,
The sweet maid next door to me.

And as the strains steal o'er me
Her moth-eyebrows rise before me.
And I feel a gentle thrill
That her fingers must be chill.

# 贫　女

[唐] 秦韬玉

蓬门未识绮罗香，拟托良媒益自伤。
谁爱风流高格调，共怜时世俭梳妆。
敢将十指夸针巧，不把双眉斗画长。
苦恨年年压金线，为他人作嫁衣裳。

【今译】

　　出身贫家未曾见过绫罗软香，想求良人说媒更暗自悲伤。谁会爱我高尚的品格和情调，都喜欢时下流行的俭妆。我敢夸我的双手灵巧擅长针线，不天天描眉与人争短长。苦恨我年复一年拿着金线刺绣，只不过是为别人赶制嫁衣罢了。

But doors and locks between us
So effectually screen us
That I hasten from the street
And in dreamland pray to meet.


## THE SEMPSTRESS

In silk and satin ne'er arrayed,
My fate to be a lone old maid;
No handsome bridegroom comes for me
Dressed in the garb of poverty.
I learned to sew with skill and grace,
Though not to paint my brows and face,
Yet I must ply my golden thread
For other maids about to wed.

## 春　夕

[唐] 催涂

水流花谢两无情，送尽东风过楚城。
胡蝶梦中家万里，子规枝上月三更。
故园书动经年绝，华发春唯满镜生。
自是不归归便得，五湖烟景有谁争。

**【今译】**

　　流水不停，花儿凋谢，这是多么无情。送最后一缕春风吹过楚城。睡梦中我回到了万里之外的家中，树上杜鹃的啼叫声惊醒了我，正是夜里三更时。家乡的来信已经长年断绝，镜子里的我已是满头白发。抱负实现后我自然就会归去了，故乡五湖的美景又有谁来与我争抢。

## 金　缕　衣

[唐] 杜秋娘

劝君莫惜金缕衣，劝君须惜少年时。
有花堪折直须折，莫待无花空折枝。

## THE TRAVELLER

The stream glides by, the flower fades,
      and neither feels a sting
That thus they pass and bear away

## GOLDEN SANDS

I would not have thee grudge those robes
      which gleam in rich array,
But I would have thee grudge the hours

古今诗选

【今译】

  劝您不要顾惜华丽的金缕衣,但要珍惜少年求学的最好时期。花开可以折取的时候要抓紧去摘,不要到花落后只折个空枝回来。

    of youth which glide away.
Go pluck the blooming flower betimes,
    lest when thou com'st again
Alas, upon the withered stem
    no blooming flowers remain!

    the glory of the spring.
I dream myself once more at home,
    a thousand miles away;
The night-jar wakes me with its cry
    ere yet 'tis early day.
Long months have passed and no word comes
    to tell me of my own;
With each New Year my scattered locks
    have white and whiter grown,
Ah my dear home, if once within
    thy threshold I could be,
The Five Lakes and their lovely scenes
    might all go hang for me.

## 旅游伤春

[唐] 李昌符

酒醒乡关远,迢迢听漏终。
曙分林影外,春尽雨声中。
鸟思江村路,花残野岸风。
十年成底事,羸马倦西东。

**【今译】**

  酒醉醒来,家乡依然遥远,远远地听着更漏声,直到天明。树林在曙色中出现倒影,春天在雨声中就要过去了。村旁的小路鸟儿在飞翔,江边的野风吹落了枝头的花朵。多年来我一事无成,像一匹瘦马一样四处奔波。

## 听 筝

[唐] 李端

鸣筝金粟柱,素手玉房前。
欲得周郎顾,时时误拂弦。

## WANDERJAHRE①

Roused from the fumes of wine, I hear the drum,
Midst thoughts of home, roll from the distant tower,
While through the trees faint streaks of daylight come,
And the spring passes in a pattering shower.

The tired bird homeward wings its way at last;
Flowers fade and die beneath wild winds oppressed.
What have my wanderings earned these ten years past?...
My wayworn horse is sick of east and west.

【注】 ①源自德语，意为"学徒期""漫游期"等。

## MUSIC HATH CHARMS

Hark to the rapturous melody!
Her white arm o'er the lute she flings...
To break her lover's reverie

【今译】

  金粟轴的古筝发出优美的声音，纤纤玉手拨弄着琴弦。想要得到周郎的关注，她不时故意拨错琴弦。

## 寄王舍人竹楼

[唐] 李嘉祐

傲吏身闲笑五侯，西江取竹起高楼。
南风不用蒲葵扇，纱帽闲眠对水鸥。

【今译】

  高傲的官吏气定神闲地笑对权贵，在西边的江岸伐竹建起了高楼。阵阵南风比蒲扇的风更舒服，在水鸥的叫声中，头戴纱帽，悠然入眠。

## 春　　怨

[唐] 刘方平

纱窗日落渐黄昏，金屋无人见泪痕。

She strikes a discord on the strings.

## IN RETIREMENT

He envies none, the pure and proud
                ex-Minister of State;
On the Western Lake he shuts himself
                within his bamboo gate.
He needs no fan to cool his brow, for
                the south wind never lulls.
While idly his official hat lies
                staring at the gulls.

## THE SPINSTER

Dim twilight throws a deeper shade

寂寞空庭春欲晚，梨花满地不开门。

【今译】

　　纱窗外太阳即将落山，黄昏渐降临，华丽的宫殿里，没人看见怨妇的泪痕。寂寞幽寂的庭院里春天已到尽头，飘落的梨花落满地，院门紧闭。

# 效崔国辅体四首(其一)

[唐] 韩　偓

　　淡月照中庭，海棠花自落。
　　独立俯闲阶，风动秋千索。

【今译】

　　淡淡的月光照着庭院中央，海棠花从枝头悄然飘落。她独自看着屋前的台阶，静听风儿吹动秋千发出的声响。

     across the window-screen;
Alone within a gilded hall
     her tear-drops flow unseen.
No sound the lonely court-yard stirs;
     the spring is all but through;
Around the pear-blooms fade and fall...
     and no one comes to woo.

## CONTEMPLATION

When my court-yard by the placid moon is lit,
When around me leaves come dropping from the trees,
On the terrace steps, contemplative, I sit,
The swing-ropes swaying idly in the breeze.

## 渡 汉 江

［唐］宋之问

岭外音书断，经冬复历春。
近乡情更怯，不敢问来人。

【今译】

　　在岭外失去了家乡的音信，经过冬天又到了春天。离故乡越近越是心生胆怯，不敢打听从故乡来的人。

## 陇 西 行

［唐］陈陶

誓扫匈奴不顾身，五千貂锦丧胡尘。
可怜无定河边骨，犹是春闺梦里人。

【今译】

　　将士们发誓横扫匈奴，个个都奋不顾身，五千名身穿锦袍的将士战死沙场。可怜无定河边那成堆的白骨，他们生前都是少妇春闺思念的梦中人。

## HOMEWARD

No letters to the frontier come,
The winter softens into spring...
I tremble as I draw near home,
And dare not ask what news you bring.

## AN OATH

They swore the Huns should perish:
    they would die if needs they must...
And now five thousand, sable-clad,
    have bit the Tartar dust.
Along the river-bank their bones
    lie scattered where they may,
But still their forms in dreams arise
    to fair ones far away.

## 寄　人

[唐] 张泌

别梦依依到谢家，小廊回合曲阑斜。
多情只有春庭月，犹为离人照落花。

【今译】

　　离别后依依不舍，又在梦里来到谢家，那里小廊曲折、栏杆横斜。只有庭中的春月最是多情，还为离人照亮庭院里的落花。

## 归　隐

[宋] 陈抟

十年踪迹走红尘，回首青山入梦频。
紫陌纵荣争及睡，朱门虽贵不如贫。
愁闻剑戟扶危主，闷见笙歌聒醉人。
携取旧书归旧隐，野花啼鸟一般春。

【今译】

　　在尘世间游历已经十年了，回头再看，青山时常出现在

## TO AN ABSENT FAIR ONE

After parting, dreams possessed me
      and I wandered you know where,
And we sat in the verandah
      and you sang the sweet old air.
Then I woke, with no one near me
      save the moon still shining on,
And lighting up dead petals
      which like you have passed and gone.

## DISILLUSIONED

For ten long years I plodded through
      the vale of lust and strife,
Then through my dreams there flashed a ray
      of the old sweet peaceful life...
No scarlet-tasselled hat of state
      can vie with soft repose;
Grand mansions do not taste the joys

门中。高官厚禄都比不上安稳的睡眠，豪门虽然富贵却不如安贫乐道。最发愁听到战乱和君王更替的消息，最苦闷听到笙歌让人醉生梦死。还是带上我的旧书退隐田园，看着野花听着鸟鸣，欣赏大自然的春光美景。

# 夜宿山寺

〔唐〕李白

危楼高百尺，手可摘星辰。
不敢高声语，恐惊天上人。

【今译】

　　山上寺院好像有百丈高，仿佛伸手就能摘到天上的星星。不敢在这里大声说话哟，说不定会惊动天上的神仙。

        that the poor man's cabin knows.
I hate the threatening clash of arms
        when fierce retainers throng,
I loathe the drunkard's revels and
        the sound of fife and song;
But I love to seek a quiet nook, and
        some old volume bring
Where I can see the wild flowers bloom
        and hear the birds in spring.


# 'TWIXT HEAVEN AND EARTH

Upon this tall pagoda's peak
My hands can nigh the stars enclose;
I dare not raise my voice to speak,
For fear of startling God's repose.

# 戏答元珍

[宋] 欧阳修

春风疑不到天涯,二月山城未见花。
残雪压枝犹有橘,冻雷惊笋欲抽芽。
夜闻归雁生乡思,病入新年感物华。
曾是洛阳花下客,野芳虽晚不须嗟。

【今译】

　　有些怀疑春风吹不到这遥远的地方,已是二月,却不见山城的花儿开放。残存的积雪压在枝头,尚能看到几个去年的橘子,寒日里的春雷惊醒了竹笋,似乎也要发芽。夜里听到雁叫唤起了我的思乡之情,抱病进入新的一年对景色感慨万千。我也曾在洛阳欣赏盛开的牡丹花,这里的野花开得虽迟,也不必感伤嗟叹。

# CONSOLATION

The balmy breath of spring must fail
    to reach that distant spot
Where early wild-flowers do not bloom
    to cheer my exile's lot.
See how the oranges still hang
    amid the clinging snow,
And shoots and buds, benumbed by cold,
    around reluctant grow!
At night your heart is with your home
    when you hear the wild goose cry.
And your sadness ever deepens
    as the smiling months go by.
Yet when you think of happy hours
    at Loyang in the past,
Grieve not that spring is late, but joy
that spring is yours at last.

# 插 花 吟

[宋] 邵雍

头上花枝照酒卮①,酒卮中有好花枝。
身经两世太平日,眼见四朝全盛时。
况复筋骸粗康健,那堪时节正芳菲。
酒涵花影红光溜,争忍花前不醉归。

【今译】

　　头上的花枝映入酒杯,酒杯中就有了好花枝。经历了六十年的太平日子,亲眼见证了四个朝代的盛世。况且我的身体还很健康,又喜逢春光明媚的芳菲时节。酒杯里的花影红光流溢,怎么舍得在花前不喝醉就回家呢。

【注】　①卮(zhī):古代一种器皿,常用来盛酒。

## A STRUGGLE

Fair flowers from above in my goblet are
                                        shining,
And add by reflection an infinite zest;
Through two generations I've lived,
                                        unrepining,
While four mighty rulers have sunk to
                                        their rest.
My body in health has done nothing to
                                        spite me,
And sweet are the moments which pass
                                        o'er my head;
But now, with this wine and these flowers
                                        to delight me,
How shall I keep sober and get home
                                        to bed?

## 有 约

[宋] 司马光

黄梅时节家家雨,青草池塘处处蛙。
有约不来过夜半,闲敲棋子落灯花。

【今译】

　　黄梅时节家家户户都笼罩在雨中,池塘边青草丛中处处传来蛙鸣。半夜时分了,邀请的客人还没有到来,我手拿棋子敲着桌面,震落了油灯的灯花。

## 清 明

[宋] 黄庭坚

佳节清明桃李笑,野田荒冢只生愁。
雷惊天地龙蛇蛰,雨足郊原草木柔。
人乞祭余骄妾妇,士甘焚死不公侯。
贤愚千载知谁是,满眼蓬蒿共一丘。

【今译】

　　清明时节桃李含笑盛开,田野上的荒坟令人感到凄凉。

## WAITING

'Tis the festival of Yellow Plums!
        the rain unceasing pours,
And croaking bullfrogs hoarsely wake
        the echoes out of doors.
I sit and wait for him in vain,
        while midnight hours go by,
And push about the chessmen
        till the lamp-wick sinks to die.

## ANNUAL WORSHIP AT TOMBS

The peach and plum trees smile with flowers
        this famous day of spring,
And country graveyards round about
        with lamentations ring.
Thunder has startled insect life
        and roused the gnats and bees,
A gentle rain has urged the crops

古今诗选

滚滚春雷惊醒了蛰伏的龙蛇百虫,春雨充沛,滋润了郊原旷野,草木变得青绿柔美。古有齐人向扫墓者乞讨祭祀后留下的酒饭,却和妻妾炫耀是富人请他喝酒,而高尚的介子推宁愿被烧死也不肯做公侯。谁贤谁愚,千百年来谁知道呢,最终都被掩埋在长满野草的坟丘中。

# 夜　直

[宋] 王安石

金炉香尽漏声残,翦翦轻风阵阵寒。
春色恼人眠不得,月移花影上栏干。

【今译】

　　香炉里的香已燃成灰烬,夜漏里的水即将滴完,微风轻柔,带着阵阵寒意。春天的夜晚让人彻夜难眠,花影随着月亮的移动,悄悄地爬上了栏杆。

  and soothed the flowers and trees...
Perhaps on this side lie the bones
  of a wretch whom no one knows;
On that, the sacred ashes
  of a patriot repose.
But who across the centuries
  can hope to mark each spot
Where fool or hero, joined in death,
  beneath the brambles rot?

# A WHITE NIGHT

The incense-stick is burnt to ash,
  the water-clock is stilled,
The midnight breeze blows sharply by
  and all around is chilled.
Yet I am kept from slumber
  by the beauty of the spring:
Sweet shapes of flowers across the blind
  the quivering moonbeams fling!

古今诗选

## 题淮南寺

[宋] 程颢

南去北来休便休，白蘋吹尽楚江秋。
道人不是悲秋客，一任晚山相对愁。

【今译】

　　南去北来没有羁扰，想休息就休息，秋风吹落了楚江里的白蘋。我可不是那伤感秋天的过客，任凭山峦在黄昏中相对愁悲。

## 春日偶成

[宋] 程颢

云淡风轻近午天，傍花随柳过前川。
时人不识余心乐，将谓偷闲学少年。

【今译】

　　时近春日的中午，微风吹动淡淡的白云，伴着鲜花和碧柳，我来到河边。旁人不知道我心里的快乐，还说我忙里偷闲，学那闲逛的少年。

# INSOUCIANCE

I wander north, I wander south,
        I rest me where I please...
See how the river-banks are nipped
        beneath the autumn breeze!
Yet what care I if autumn blasts
        the river-banks lay bare?
The loss of hue to river-banks
        is the river-banks' affair.

# SPRING FANCIES

When clouds are thin, and the wind is light,
        about the noontide hour,
I cross the stream, through willow paths
        with all around in flower.
The world knows not my inmost thoughts
        which make me seem a fool;
I'm taken for a truant boy
        escaped from tedious school.

## 春　宵

[宋] 苏轼

春宵一刻值千金，花有清香月有阴。
歌管楼台声细细，秋千院落夜沉沉。

【今译】

　　春天的夜晚，一刻就价值千金，花儿散发着淡淡的清香，月光投射下阴影。远处楼台传来隐约的舞乐歌声，挂着秋千的庭院笼罩在夜色之中。

## 花　影

[宋] 苏轼

重重叠叠上瑶台，几度呼童扫不开。
刚被太阳收拾去，又叫明月送将来。

【今译】

　　花影一层又一层映照在亭台，几次叫书童去打扫却怎么也扫不开。好不容易等到太阳落山，花影不见了，可是月亮升起，花影又重新出现。

## SPRING NIGHTS

One half-hour of a night in spring
        is worth a thousand taels,
When the clear sweet scent of flowers is felt
        and the moon her lustre pales;
When mellowed sounds of song and flute
        are borne along the breeze,
And through the stilly scene the swing
        sounds swishing from the trees.

## WHIGS AND TORIES

Thickly o'er the jasper terrace
        flower shadows play;
In vain I call my garden boy
        to sweep them all away.
They vanish when the sun sets
        in the west, but very soon
They spring to giddy life again
        beneath the rising moon!

古今诗选

## 秋 千

[宋] 洪觉范

画架双裁翠络偏,佳人春戏小楼前。
飘扬血色裙拖地,断送玉容人上天。
花板润沾红杏雨,彩绳斜挂绿杨烟。
下来闲处从容立,疑是蟾宫谪降仙。

【今译】

　　秋千架上挂的彩绳飘向高空,是美女在春天于小楼前戏耍。飘舞的红色裙边掠过了地面,秋千又将美女荡上了青天。美女的汗珠像杏花瓣,雨点般飘落在秋千的踏板上,彩绳恰如轻烟飘浮在杨柳中间。美女从秋千下来后气定神闲,从容站立,真好似那月宫里的仙女降到了人间。

## SWINGING

Two green silk ropes, with painted stand,
        from heights aerial swing,
And there outside the house a maid
        disports herself in spring.
Along the ground her blood-red skirts
        all swiftly swishing fly,
As though to bear her off to be
        an angel in the sky,
Strewed thick with fluttering almond-blooms
        the painted stand is seen;
The embroidered ropes flit to and fro
        amid the willow green.
Then when she stops and out she springs
        to stand with downcast eyes,
You think she is some angel
        just now banished from the skies.

古今诗选

## 初夏游张园

[宋] 戴复古

乳鸭池塘水浅深,熟梅天气半阴晴。
东园载酒西园醉,摘尽枇杷一树金。

【今译】

　　小鸭子在池塘里或浅或深的水里游来游去,梅子成熟的时节,天气忽晴忽阴。大家载酒醉游了东园又游西园,信手摘下满园树上金黄的枇杷。

## 游园不值

[宋] 叶绍翁

应怜屐齿印苍苔,小扣柴扉久不开。
春色满园关不住,一枝红杏出墙来。

【今译】

　　大概是园主担心我的木屐踩上了青苔,我轻敲柴门久久没人来开。可是满园的春色终究是关不住的,一枝红色的杏花悄然伸出了墙外。

## SUMMER

When ducklings seek the puddles, mostly dry,
In the hot plum-time, with its changeful sky,
'Tis then in shady artdur we carouse,
And strip the golden loquat from the boughs.

## AT A PARK GATE

'Tis closed! — lest trampling footsteps mar
    the glory of the green.
Time after time we knock and knock;
    no janitor is seen.
Yet bolts and bars can't quite shut in
    the spring-time's beauteous pall:
A pink-flowered almond-spray peeps out
    athwart the envious wall!

## 冷　泉

〔宋〕林洪

一泓清可沁诗脾，冷暖年来只自知。
流出西湖载歌舞，回头不是在山时。

【今译】

　　一片清凉的泉水沁人心脾，年复一年或冷或暖，只有泉水自己知道。泉水流进西湖，承载着歌舞升平的游船，回头再看，自己已不像深山时纯洁清澈了。

## 送　春

〔宋〕王逢原

三月残花落更开，小檐日日燕飞来。
子规夜半犹啼血，不信东风唤不回。

【今译】

　　三月里的花儿败了又开，小小的屋檐下燕子天天飞来。子规鸟到了半夜仍然啼叫不止，它不相信东风召唤不回来。

## A MOUNTAIN BROOK

One draught for my poetic soul I take,
Unconscious river, ere thou glid'st away
To serve the orgies of the Western Lake,
And be no more the pure stream of today.

## THE THIRD MOON

In May flowers fade, and others come
        to bloom among the leaves,
While all day long the nesting swallow
        flits around the eaves.
The night-jar cries half through the night
        until the blood flows fast.
Ah vainly hoping to recall the
        spring that now is past!

古今诗选

# 清明日对酒

[宋] 高翥

南北山头多墓田,清明祭扫各纷然。
纸灰飞作白蝴蝶,泪血染成红杜鹃。
日落狐狸眠冢上,夜归儿女笑灯前。
人生有酒须当醉,一滴何曾到九泉!

【今译】

　　南北的山上有很多墓地,清明节那天都是上坟祭扫的人。烧的纸灰像是白色的蝴蝶四处飞舞,亲人的血泪染红了满山的杜鹃。太阳落山后,只有狐狸在坟地里睡觉,归家后的儿女们在油灯前笑谈。人生在世,今朝有酒今朝醉,百年后祭祀的酒一滴也到不了九泉。

## WORSHIP, AND AFTER

The northern and the southern hills
    are one large burying-ground,
And all is life and bustle there
    when the sacred day comes round.
Burnt paper cash, like butterflies,
    fly fluttering far and wide,
While mourners' robes with tears of blood
    a crimson hue are dyed.
The sun sets, and the red fox crouches
    down beside the tomb;
Night comes, and youths and maidens laugh
    where lamps light up the gloom.
Let him, whose fortune brings him wine,
    get tipsy while he may;
For no man, when the long night comes,
    can take one drop away!

## 蚕妇吟

〔宋〕谢枋得

子规啼彻四更时,起视蚕稠怕叶稀。
不信楼头杨柳月,玉人歌舞未曾归。

【今译】

　　四更时分,子规鸟在窗外不停地啼叫,蚕妇起床看看蚕宝宝,怕桑叶太少不够吃。听到远处月下的楼台传来歌舞之声,歌女们仍在歌舞,还未归家。

## 暮春即事

〔宋〕叶采

双双瓦雀行书案,点点杨花入砚池。
闲坐小窗读周易,不知春去几多时。

【今译】

　　房瓦上一对麻雀的影子在书桌上不断移动,屋外片片杨花随风飘到屋里落进了砚池。我气定神闲坐在小窗下研读《周易》,浑然不知春天已经过去了多久。

## AT HIS CLUB

Long past midnight the wife hears
    the goatsucker's cry,
And rises to see that the
    silkworms are fed;
Alas! there's the moon shining
    low in the sky,
But her husband has not yet
    come back to his bed.

## AT HIS BOOKS

Shadows of pairing sparrows cross his book,
Of poplar catkins, dropping overhead...
The weary student from his window-nook
Looks up to find that spring is long since dead.

## 晨诣祥符寺

[明] 刘基

上马鸡始鸣，入寺钟未歇。
草际起微风，林端淡斜月。
僧房湛幽寂，假寐待明发。
松径断无人，经声在清樾。

【今译】

　　出发时鸡才叫第一遍，到了古寺晨钟尚在敲。阵阵微风掠过草地，树林上头月亮还斜挂在天空。僧人的房舍沉浸在一片寂静中，还能打一会盹到天亮再走。松间小道上没有一个人，诵经的声音在树荫下隐约传来。

## 绝　　句

[明] 刘基

人生无百岁，百岁复如何？
古来英雄士，各已归山河。

【今译】

　　人生在世很难活到一百岁，即使活到又能如何呢？自古以来的英雄壮士，都已经死去归入了江河之中。

## AT A MOUNTAIN MONASTERY

I mounted when the cock had just begun,
And reached the convent ere the bells were done.
A gentle zephyr whispered o'er the lawn;
Behind the wood the moon gave way to dawn.
And in this pure sweet solitude I lay,
Stretching my limbs out to await the day,
No sound along the willow pathway dim
Save the soft echo of the bonzes' hymn.

## OMNES EODEM[①]

A centenarian 'mongst men
Is rare; and if one comes, what then?
The mightiest heroes of the past
Upon the hillside sleep at last.

【注】 ①此标题为拉丁文,意思是"全都一样"。

古今诗选

# 暮春江上送别

［明］赵彩姬

一片潮声下石头，江亭送客使人愁。
可怜垂柳丝千尺，不为春江绾去舟。

【今译】

　　在阵阵潮声中您要去南京，江边亭子里为您送别使我心生忧愁。江边垂下的柳丝纵然有千尺之长，也挽留不住这江上您乘坐的小舟。

# 送毛伯温

［明］朱厚熜

大将生来胆气豪，腰横秋水雁翎刀。
风吹鼍鼓山河动，电闪旌旗日月高。
天上麒麟原有种，穴中蝼蚁岂能逃。
太平待诏归来日，朕与先生解战袍。

【今译】

　　将军天生豪迈有胆气，腰挎秋水般明亮的钢刀。风中战

## TO HER LOVER

The tide in the river beginning to rise,
Near the sad hour of parting, brings tears
                      to our eyes;
Alas that these furlongs of willow-strings
                      gay
Cannot hold fast the boat that will soon
                      be away!


## TO GENERAL MAO

Southward, in all the panoply
        of cruel war arrayed,
See, Our heroic general points
        and waves his glittering blade!
Across the hills and streams
        the lizard-drums terrific roll,
While glint of myriad banners

古今诗选

鼓响起,山河震动,天空中的闪电将战旗照亮。将军是天上麒麟的后代,洞穴中的蝼蚁岂是你的对手。等到天下太平将军奉召回朝的时候,我亲自为将军解下战袍。

flashes high from pole to pole...
Go, scion of the Unicorn,
  and prove thy heavenly birth.
And crush to all eternity
  these insects of the earth;
And when thou com'st, a conqueror,
  from those wild barbarian lands.
We will unhitch thy war-cloak
  with Our own Imperial hands!